CW00847862

SECONDS OUT
RUBY SCOTT

Copyright © 2020, Ruby Scott

This is a work of fiction. The characters and events portrayed in the book are fictitious. Any resemblance to actual persons, living or dead, businesses and events is purely coincidental.

No part of this book may be reproduced, or stored in a retrieval system, or transmitted in any form or by any means, electronic, mechanical, photocopying, recording, or otherwise, without express written permission. For permissions, contact RubyScott.author@gmail.com

"The individual has always had to struggle to keep from being overwhelmed by the tribe. If you try it, you will be lonely often, and sometimes frightened. But no price is too high to pay for the privilege of owning yourself."

- Friedrich Nietzsche

"Be yourself, everyone else is taken."

- Oscar Wilde

CONTENTS

One

The first time Abs saw the kid who lived across the hall from her mom, she thought nothing of her. Neighbors seemed to come and go, but her mum, who had lived here since Abs had left home twelve years ago, never seemed to mind. Abs and the girl just nodded to each other like how neighbors do and then went their separate ways. She barely even registered the full bag of groceries that hung in the girl's hand, but when she thought about it later, she realized it was another one of those signs that she should have picked up on much sooner.

But she didn't. She didn't pick up on the signs, no matter how glaringly obvious they should have been—to her, of all people. When she saw the girl coming home after dark on her own, Abs just assumed she was mature for her age. She just thought she was a 'good kid'. Quiet and respectful, and always willing to help her parents.

It wasn't until garbage day when Abs suspected something was up. She offered to take the trash out for her mom on her way out of the building, and that was when she spotted the girl from across the hall. *Gracie*, her mom had said her name was. She was coming out of her own apartment with a black garbage bag in her hands, practically dragging it along the floor because it was too heavy. Gracie closed the door behind her, and hoisted the bag up with both hands to carry it as she headed towards the stairs. As she did so, Abs heard a noise coming from inside the girl's bag.

The hollow sound of glass knocking against glass.

The sound caught Abs's attention as she followed behind the girl towards the stairwell—a gentle clink as the bag swayed with every footstep. It was unmistakable.

Sure, it could have been something else; it could have been jars of pasta sauce, or glass milk bottles, or a bunch of other things. It wasn't necessarily bottles of alcohol.

But it sure *sounded* like it. It sounded exactly like those bags Abs would haul out to the recycling late at night as a teenager, long after her father had passed out in an armchair with his mouth open in a snore.

Abs followed the teenager down to the garbage disposal. There wasn't a trash chute in her mom's building, so all the residents had to go to the first floor to dump their garbage in the dumpster by the alley. The two walked down the stairwell in silence, with Gracie leading the way until they reached the fire escape door that led outside.

"You want me to take that out for you?" Abs offered. She knew the dumpster was close enough so the girl could most likely just throw it in, but she felt bad for the kid. She knew how heavy those garbage bags could be when you were young, especially after lugging them down three flights of stairs.

Gracie looked around in surprise, as though she'd somehow forgotten that Abs was there. She looked her up and down, a little suspiciously, before finally nodding.

"Sure."

Abs bent down to grab the bag from Gracie's hand, lifting it up easily. It was heavy, but she managed to lift it as though it weighed nothing at all.

"Mind holding the door open for me?" Abs asked, before stepping out into the alleyway.

The chilly night air bit at her face as Abs stepped out into the darkness between the apartment building and the weak light that hung over the dumpster. With the ease and grace of someone who'd done this a hundred times before, Abs swung the first bag up and into the dumpster, closely followed by the second.

Before stepping back into the building, Abs looked up and down the dark alley. To her left, the alley led out onto the street where the distant lamps cast an orange glow. To her right, the alley came to an abrupt dead end where the building stopped. She couldn't even tell how far back that

2

was though, because none of the lights stretched that far. Beyond the circle of light that came from the open fire escape, the rest of the alley was an inky dark void.

Yeah, Abs decided. She definitely wouldn't have let her own teenage daughter, if she had one, down here to take out the trash at night. Hell, she didn't even feel that safe out here.

"You coming in?" Gracie called from the doorway. "Or should I just leave you out there?"

"I'm coming." Abs drew her gaze from the darkness of the alley and turned back to Gracie, who was waiting for her, half hanging out of the doorway. Abs stepped back inside, letting the door swing shut behind her, and double checked that it had locked.

The two began walking back up the staircase towards their floor, side by side, in an uncomfortable silence. Gracie had her hands stuffed deep into the pockets of her jeans, with her head bent down low to avoid eye contact.

"You're Gracie, right?" Abs said finally. The teenager just nodded silently. "I'm Maria's daughter, Abby, but everyone calls me Abs."

"Oh, right?" Gracie's voice sounded distant, like she wasn't even really paying attention. "Fire."

"Guess that makes us sort of like neighbors, huh?" Abs chuckled nervously. She had no children of her own, and no siblings either, which meant no young nieces or nephews. She always felt so hopeless at talking to anyone under the age of eighteen.

"Do you live with your mom?" Gracie asked.

"Well, no," Abs admitted.

"Then we're not neighbors," Gracie said flatly.

Shit, okay, kid. Fuck me for trying to make conversation then.

"I guess not," Abs agreed, deciding it was best to just keep her mouth shut. Gracie clearly didn't want to talk, and it was understandable. If she was a teenager, she probably wouldn't have wanted to talk to the weird, friendly adult daughter of her neighbor, either.

As they reached their floor, Gracie turned to Abs, looking her in the eyes. "Thanks for doing that."

"No problem." Abs offered a friendly smile; one Gracie didn't bother returning. "I'll see you around, I guess."

"Yeah. See you around." Gracie walked past Abs to get to her apartment. She pushed the door open – not much, just enough to slip inside – and then the door closed and latched behind her.

Abs unlocked the door to her mom's apartment and wandered inside, kicking off her shoes by the doorway. Her mom was right where she'd left her, bustling around the kitchen.

"I bumped into that kid again. What are you doing?"

"Nothing," her mom called out, her head halfway into one of the cupboards. "What kid?"

"The kid from across the hall. Gracie."

Abs narrowed her eyes as she took a step towards her mother. Although the layout of her apartment kitchen was different to the kitchen of Abs's childhood home, her mother was a slave to routine, and she'd organized her kitchen in much the same way as her old one. That was why Abs knew, without even looking into the cupboard, that her mother was hunting for baking supplies. The cupboard to the right of the stove had always been reserved for baking trays, cake tins, mixing bowls and scales. *Always*.

"Are you baking something?"

Her mother paused and drew her head out of the cupboard meekly. "Maybe."

"Don't you dare. You know what the doctor said." Abs pointed down to the cast on her mother's right hand, the one she'd been sporting for two weeks now. "No lifting or strain. Let it heal."

4

"But you've been doing so much for me the past couple of weeks. I just wanted to give you something—as a thank you."

"You can thank me by *not* damaging your wrist any more than it already is." Abs helped her mother up off the kitchen floor with a smile, before pulling her sleeve back. "You don't want to end up like me, do you?"

She held her hand up, wiggling her fingers. Under the bright kitchen lights, the thin scars that ran along her thumb and index finger showed up clearly against her tanned skin.

"Okay, okay." Her mother waved her away with her one good hand. "I get your point. I won't do anything for myself, I'll just sit here like some old woman, waiting for my daughter to take care of me. You may as well just throw me in a home right now."

"Okay." Abs grinned. "You want me to drop you off on my way home?"

A broken wrist wasn't the end of the world. In fact, it wasn't even the end of the year—the doctors had assured her mom that she should only need the cast for eight weeks, maybe even a little less. But of course, in the meantime, it meant that she needed to rely on her daughter to do things like carry the laundry down to the basement, or take out the heavy garbage bags that she needed two hands for. Even baking with her heavy trays and thick glass mixing bowls would strain her wrist.

Perhaps that stubbornness was woven deep into her mother's DNA, though. After all, Abs had been the same after the operation on her hand, and still stubbornly claimed that it wasn't as bad as the doctors had made it out to be.

"Anyway," her mom said, eager to change the subject. "You said you saw Gracie?"

"Yeah, she was taking out the garbage for her parents." Abs paused, thinking about the sound of bottles clinking together inside the garbage bag. Maybe she was just being paranoid. Maybe she was just projecting her own childhood memories onto the girl and her family.

"It's her father that lives across the hall." Abs's mother scowled at the door, like she could see through it and into the other apartment. "Her parents are divorced. And it's no surprise why."

"Not a fan of your next-door neighbor?" Abs asked, leaning on the kitchen counter. There was a pause, while her mother struggled to find the right way to express just why she found the man so intolerable.

"Ed reminds me—of your father." It was the only way she could sum it up, but it was enough. More than enough, in fact, for Abs to understand; not just her mother's expression, but Gracie's behavior.

Suddenly, coming home with grocery shopping made sense. Getting herself to and from school alone, even though this wasn't exactly a safe part of the city, made sense. She wasn't just a 'good kid'. She wasn't just 'mature for her age,' or any of the other ways that Abs herself had been described when she was growing up.

"Oh," was all she could say.

"Hmm." Her mother nodded with a sigh. "If anything, he's worse than your father. I mean, at least *he* seemed to care about your well-being. But Ed...I don't know, maybe I'm judging him too hastily. But whenever I talk to him about Gracie, he just seems so...cold."

"Poor kid," Abs said quietly, looking back towards the door she'd just come through. She couldn't help but feel just a little guilty for overlooking the signs. Gracie wasn't helping out with chores when she took the garbage out; she didn't have a choice in the matter. She wasn't mature for her age when she picked up groceries after school; she just knew that if she didn't, she would go hungry.

Two

It was cold when Abs woke up the next morning. She knew that before she'd even gotten out of bed, just from how stiff her hands were. Her hands always ached in the mornings; maybe it was something about not using them for a few hours, however, cold mornings were always the worst. It hurt to even clench them into fists.

Most of the time, it was pretty easy for Abs to forget about the injury that had cut her career so short. The vast majority of the time, the injury was little more than a scar she could catch in certain lights, and a pain when she worked out on the punching bags for too long. But the mornings were a sharp reminder.

She hauled herself out of bed with a grunt, wincing as her bare feet hit the cold floorboards. Yeah, it was a cold morning.

Holding onto a hot cup of coffee helped some mornings, so her first stop was the kitchen. She barely held back a yawn as the coffee machine whirred away, and when it was ready, she curled the fingers of her right hand around it, closing her eyes as she waited for some pain and stiffness to subside.

Her mom had joked on more than one occasion that Abs was more of an old woman than she was. Right now, hunched over the kitchen countertop trying to ease her aching wrists, she certainly *felt* like an arthritic senior.

Twenty-nine years old with the hands of a seventy year old.

The first cup of coffee didn't do much to ease the pain in her hand, and neither did the second. A firm massage while scowling at her hand helped a little, but almost as soon as she pulled her good hand away and the pressure was gone, the pain returned.

So it was going to be one of *those* days.

7

Reluctantly, Abs pulled out the compression glove her mom had bought her, from the back of the closet where she'd stuffed it. She'd always been too stubborn to get herself one, sneering at the 'perfect for arthritis' label on the packaging; she wasn't actually riddled with arthritis, as much as everyone joked about it. But her mom had bought it for her, and as much as she hated to admit it, the glove helped on the bad days.

She pulled it on, wincing as the fabric tightened around her fingers. It limited her mobility a little, but hell, on a morning like this, her mobility was limited anyway. Abs clenched her hand into a fist experimentally, only managing to close it loosely before it became too painful to do so. If she couldn't even form a proper fist, work was going to be hard.

"Hell," Abs whispered to herself. "I guess I'm on desk duty then."

Sapphy's gym was fast earning itself a reputation as one of the best all womens gym in the city, and it was only a ten minute drive from Abs's place. Built in the remnants of an old warehouse, it wasn't much to look at from the outside.

The painted brick walls were cool in a sort of run-down industrial hipster kind of way, but to an outsider it might have just looked a little unloved and underfunded. Even the sign above the heavy metal door that bore the gym's name was beginning to fade. But rather than replace Sapphy, who owned the gym, she claimed it added to the aesthetic.

Abs passed by the reception desk in the lobby—today manned by Shannon, the sweet college student who was more of a cardio bunny than a boxer. She was scrolling through her phone when Abs pushed the heavy, dark gray door open. The whoosh of air that followed Abs into the building caused Shannon to look up, and then she quickly fumbled to hide the phone out of sight. Realizing it was only Abs though, she relaxed.

"Morning, Abs," she called out, waving at her. Abs held up her good hand in a wave, smiling gently.

"You should put that thing away, you know."

"I don't use it when the clients come in," she assured, without looking up from her phone.

"You'd better not, and don't let Sapphy catch you or she'll find more stuff to keep you busy." Abs smiled gently, before heading through the double doors that led into the gym where she could hear the faint sounds of a few early birds already working out.

Her office was next to Sapphy's, up a flight of stairs to the side of the main floor of the gym. The big windows gave a great view of the main floor, from the boxing ring itself to the punching bags and speed bags that were suspended along the far wall.

Abs threw herself down into her chair with a heavy sigh, looking at the calendar on her desk. She had three private classes today, including one before lunch, and she knew she wouldn't be able to teach any of them with her hand hurting like this.

Her gaze shifted from the calendar to the framed photograph beside it. It was an old picture—taken when she was still competing. Her arm was slung around the shoulder of a taller woman with rich, tanned skin, her hair pulled back from her face in a tight bun. Abs herself had hair even shorter than what it was now, and it was her natural color—a mousy brown—it looked alien to her now, given she'd dyed it blonde in recent years. A medal hung around her neck.

Both women were flushed, dripping with sweat, and even in the photograph Abs could tell they were exhausted. The photo had been taken mere seconds after they'd both clambered out of the ring, and even though they were both tired, they looked happy. They were beaming at the camera.

It was the only match she'd ever fought against her best friend, Sapphy. They had been in the same weight class back when Abs had fought in the ring, and they had attended college in the same city. With a shared competitive spirit and 'work hard, play hard' attitude, it took no one by surprise

9

when they quickly became close friends. Although they'd always fought matches in the same circles and shared many of the same opponents, it took years before they went up against each other. Sapphy had transitioned more into Muay Thai for a while too, but it was a move that Abs had wanted to follow.

It was an odd thing, to want to pummel your best friend into the mat, but Abs could still remember just how excited they'd both been to fight each other. It had been the most fun she'd had during training, and when the match was over, she gladly slung her arms around her best friend's neck and laughed. They'd both talked about a rematch in the next season, and Sapphy had promised her that the next time they fought, she'd win.

They never got a rematch. That picture was taken only a couple of weeks before the car accident, and it was one of the last fights Abs ever had.

When Abs had been in the accident, Sapphy had been there for her. She'd arrived at the hospital before Abs's own mother, after hearing about it from some other friends who'd been in the area at the time. When the pain meds had kicked in, she was the one to make a note of everything her friend had said, and when the meds had worn off, she had been the one to gather Abs up in her arms and cuddle her.

She was a rock, a constant. Of course, Abs's mom had been there by her side too, and Abs was forever grateful for that, but her mother's sympathy couldn't compare to Sapphy's empathy. Abs felt like she had to put on a brave face for her mom's sake, but with Sapphy, she'd been able to cry, scream, mourn. And she'd done all of those things. They had been through so much together that when Sapphy had asked her to be her right hand in her new gym, Abs had immediately said yes.

She was in charge of training staff and dealt with much of the day to day minutiae, which Sapphy didn't care for, as well as head up training classes herself.

My right hand...

The irony of Sapphy's words rang in Abs's ears. Pulling her phone from her pocket, she winced as her fingers curled around it. Yeah, there was no way she was going to be able to teach classes with her hand like this.

Need you in my office ASAP.

She sent the text to Logan before tossing her phone on the desk, massaging the thumb and forefinger in an attempt to ease the aching. It hadn't been this bad in a long time, and normally by now the pain would have subsided enough that Abs would be able to get on with her day. But apparently today she'd managed to seriously piss off some magic karmic being, and this was her punishment.

Logan walked in without bothering to knock, just like always. As she came into her office, Abs sat upright, dropping her hand on the desk. Logan didn't need to see how much pain she was in.

"You called, oh fearless leader?" Logan dropped into the chair across from Abs with a smile.

While Abs was officially second in command, she never lauded that position over anyone. They were a team and to make it work, everyone had to work together and pull their weight. In turn, that meant she was open to as much teasing as any of the other instructors.

"I've got a few classes today that I'll need you to take, if you can. Reggie Thompson has a match in a couple of weeks. She was going to spend a couple of hours working with me. Then I've got two classes with some rookies in the afternoon. Can you pick them up for me?"

"Why d'you need me to take them?" Logan asked. Of course, it would have been too much to hope that Logan would just accept the job without asking questions.

"Busy day." Abs lied, shrugging. "Sapphy wants me to get the staffing budgets done for next quarter, and I need to get a head start."

11

"Is that right?" Logan cocked her head to one side, looking her friend up and down slowly. "It wouldn't have anything to do with that compression glove on your hand, would it?"

Abs slipped her hand from the desk to her lap quickly, even though she knew it was too late. Logan had seen it, and she'd known Abs long enough to put two and two together. But still, she gave it one more shot. "Nope."

Logan sighed heavily, leaning forward so her elbows rested on the desk. A line appeared between her brows as she frowned at Abs. "You know, if the pain's getting bad again—"

"It's just a little stiff, that's all."

"*If the pain's getting bad again,*" Logan repeated, a little more forcefully. "You should go see your doctor. Maybe something's wrong with the pins in your hand? You know, sometimes the body can just start rejecting implants, or there could be an infection, or—"

"Thank you, Doctor House," Abs quipped, cutting across her. She knew that Logan was trying to help, she knew that she was worried. But Abs didn't *want* her to worry. She didn't want pity either. "I'll be okay. It's just worse on the cold days."

Logan sat back, folding her arms over her chest. She didn't exactly look comforted by that, but she knew Abs was too stubborn to change her mind. "I'll take your classes, don't worry about it. But I still think you should get a second opinion from a doctor."

"Yeah, yeah." Abs smiled gently. "I get it."

She watched Logan leave, and when the door closed behind her friend, Abs leaned back in her chair again, massaging along the thin scar of her forefinger. Perhaps Logan was right. Perhaps she *did* need to go see her doctor.

Three

The pain had subsided back to normal levels by the time Abs's afternoon classes rolled around, so she spent the majority of her time after lunch watching rookie fighters stumble around the ring. Maybe to an outsider they wouldn't have looked too bad, but Abs picked up on everything. Every heavy footstep, every missed opportunity for a jab.

After she finished her last class of the day, Abs headed to her mom's place to see if there was anything she needed done in the apartment. At first, her mom was adamant that there was nothing and that Abs should just head home instead, but after a few moments of prodding her, Abs spotted the laundry hamper was close to overflowing.

"You were planning on carrying this all the way to the basement, were you?" she said pointedly, before filling up a laundry bag.

As Abs left the apartment and closed it behind her, she heard the door to Gracie's apartment open. She turned at the noise, half expecting to see Gracie at the doorway. Instead, she came face to face with a man she'd never seen before.

Ed.

He wasn't what Abs expected at all. In her head, he looked a little something like her father; unshaven, three or four days out from his last shower, and stinking of booze. She expected to see a man with bleary, red-rimmed eyes, a perpetual slur, and a beer belly.

That was nothing like how Ed really looked.

He was younger than what she had expected, maybe only ten years older than she was, and perhaps that was why he wasn't showing the signs of alcohol abuse yet. He was well groomed, clean shaven and with gelled back dark hair peppered with grays. There were circles under his eyes, sure, and his skin looked a little sickly, but to any unsuspecting passer-by that might just be considered as an office tan. He was even dressed in a casual navy suit, and must have been heading out somewhere.

A date, perhaps?

Abs's father hadn't gone on dates. He hadn't ever left the house unless it was for work. If he had gone to parties or barbecues with friends, he would have had to face the social pressure of behaving himself, of limiting how much he drank. Under the judgmental gaze of his friends and neighbors, he'd have had to pretend like he was everyone else. He'd have had to stop drinking when the others did, no matter how badly he'd have wanted to reach for that next beer.

With hindsight, Abs figured that it had been easier for him to just stay home. So maybe Ed wasn't quite there yet? Maybe he still had a few years left where he could at least feel like he was in control. But he wasn't.

"Evening." Ed paused, looking her up and down slowly. There was no mistaking the look in his eyes as they raked over Abs's body from head to toe, as if he could undress her right there in the hallway. "I don't think we've been formally introduced yet."

"Don't think we have, no."

"You must be Maria's daughter, right? Abs?"

"That's me."

Either Ed didn't pick up on the ice cold tone of Abs's voice, or simply didn't care. He didn't seem put off by her lack of enthusiasm.

"Maria didn't tell me you were so pretty."

Abs's stomach turned at those words. It was an empty, hollow compliment, probably one of the thousands in his mental cache. There was something about it that made her skin crawl—maybe just how insincere she knew it was. And *God*, she hated the way he was looking at her. He was openly ogling her, the way she'd only read about on the Let's Not Meet forum on Reddit.

14

Yeah, she got why her mom wasn't a fan.

"Are you heading down?" Ed asked, putting his hand on the banister of the stairs. He gestured out with one hand, offering her to lead.

"You go," Abs said with a tight-lipped smile, gesturing to the stairwell. "I left something back in the apartment."

"Okay." Ed smiled at her, but again there was something oddly cold about it.

The smile *should* have been perfectly normal, but it just wasn't quite right. It didn't reach his eyes the way it should have, and the effect of smiling with only half his face was deeply unnerving. He didn't move though. Didn't head for the stairs. He just hung there instead, with one hand lazily draped on the banister, like he was waiting for her to say something else.

"I'll see you around," Abs said quietly, nodding to him before turning on her heel and heading off for her mom's apartment. She hadn't forgotten anything back inside, she just didn't really feel like making small talk with Ed on the way to the basement. There was something about that smile that just screamed *fake* to her.

She ducked back into her mom's place for a few moments, giving Ed enough time to make it all the way out of the apartment building, before poking her head back out there. The hallway was empty, and there were no sounds of echoing footsteps coming from the stairwell either, so Abs felt safe heading down.

The laundry room was in the basement, and it was empty when Abs made her way down there. There weren't even any machines running, which meant she could take her time peeking inside each machine to try to find the one that was the least dirty. She really didn't trust public laundry machines.

After finding one that only looked a *little* gross, Abs tossed the laundry inside, turning it onto the longest wash she could before dusting her hands off. As the machine whirred

15

to life, she grabbed the laundry bag off the floor, and was about to head back upstairs when she heard footsteps in the stairwell.

Over the sound of the machine, Abs could hear footsteps coming down the staircase towards the laundry room, along with a weird shuffling noise. She turned to look at the door, only to see Gracie coming in. She was gripping the handle of a huge laundry bag between her hands, and it was so heavy that she was having to drag it along the floor rather than carry it. That must have been the shuffling noise Abs had heard.

"Hey," Abs said, holding up a hand in a wave.

"Hi," Gracie said quietly, shuffling past her with the laundry bag towards the row of machines against the far wall.

"You want a hand with that?" Abs asked. The kid could barely even carry it. There was no way she'd be able to lift it up to tip it into the machine.

"I'm fine." Gracie passed by her, stopping by the machine next to Abs's. She paused for a moment, and then opened the bag up, but hesitated before sticking her hand inside to grab a handful of clothes.

Why is this kid being so stubborn? Abs wondered, setting her own laundry bag down on the floor before going to help her. When she stooped down to grab the handles of the bag, though, she realized what was wrong.

As Abs got close to the bag, the putrid smell of stale alcohol hit her, and it took all of her self-control not to gag and turn her head away. God, she hadn't smelled that in a long time. That sickening mixture of alcohol and sweat ingrained into the fabric. It was a smell that would linger no matter how many times the clothing went through the wash, and it stained everything it touched.

Abs jerked the bag up easily and tipped the clothes into the drum of the machine before Gracie could reach out and stop her. As soon as the bag was empty, Gracie slammed the lid shut and snatched it from her, hugging it to her chest.

She ducked her head, avoiding Abs's gaze, and even though the lighting in the laundry room was nothing more than a sickly pale glow, she could still see Gracie's cheeks were burning. Her breathing was a little faster than normal, like she'd just been caught doing something she wasn't supposed to.

"Thanks," she said quietly.

"No problem."

Abs watched as Gracie pushed past her to get to the machine, dumping a little of the pre-provided laundry powder into the machine before turning it on.

It made sense now, all of it did.

Abs took a couple of steps back, before hopping on top of one of the unused dryers, crossing one leg over the other. Gracie kept her back to Abs, fiddling with the strap of her laundry bag, her shoulders hunched up towards her ears.

"It sucks, doesn't it?" Abs asked. "Living with someone like that."

For a few moments, Gracie was quiet, and the only sound in the room was the low hum of their washing machines whirring. She turned just a little, so that Abs could see her face, and even though her mouth opened like she was about to say something, no words came out. Instead, she just stared wordlessly into the middle distance, a frown creasing her features.

Abs wondered if anyone had talked to her about this before. Maybe no one had noticed. Maybe they had, but they just hadn't put two and two together. Perhaps, just like Abs, they had simply dismissed Gracie as little more than a 'good kid'.

"I remember what it was like," Abs continued. "Growing up in a house with a father who acted more like a kid than what I did."

Gracie looked over at her slowly, a little uncertainly, like she was trying to judge exactly what it was that Abs wanted from her. Her grip on the laundry bag tightened a little, her fingers curling into the coarse fabric.

"You do?" she said quietly, and at those words, Abs felt her heart break just a little. The teenager sounded so hopeful, like she'd just been offered a lifeline.

Was this really the first time anyone had reached out to Gracie? She hadn't told anyone?

Abs managed a small smile for Gracie's benefit. "Yeah. I do."

"Your dad was like mine?"

"Sure seems like it, yeah. And my mom, she was working really long hours, so she couldn't really help out. I got left home with him a lot."

"My mom works long hours too," Gracie said quietly. "She's an emergency dispatcher, so she works a lot of nights."

"Is that why you're here with your dad?"

"Yeah, they divorced years ago. Mum thought I should keep contact with him and when they changed her contract, so she had to work more nights, she thought it would be better for me," Gracie said, dropping the empty laundry bag to the floor.

"Does she know what he's like?"

Gracie offered up a non-committal shrug. "I guess so. But he's gotten worse. Did your mom know what your dad was like?"

"Yeah, she knew. They stayed together, but she didn't have much of a choice when it came to leaving me at home with him. It was either that or quit her job—given she was the only one bringing money in…" Abs shrugged.

After a moment's thought, Gracie hopped up onto the dryer beside Abs, swinging her legs lazily. That frown was still on her face as she stared into the middle distance, obviously deep in thought. A few moments later, she spoke up.

"Did your dad get better?"

18

She knew what Gracie was really asking. She wanted to hear that her dad had gotten better, because maybe – just maybe – there would be a hope for her own dad. Maybe she'd be able to get her dad back. Maybe she wouldn't have to buy her groceries from the corner store on her way home from school, or do her father's laundry after he passed out on the couch. She could be a kid again.

Abs wished she could say yes.

As it turned out though, she didn't have to say anything at all. It must have been written all over her face, because Gracie looked away with a disappointed sigh.

"He died when I was just a little older than you are now," Abs admitted, feeling a little guilty as she saw Gracie's shoulder's slump.

Perhaps she should have lied, or at least tried to soften the truth.

"I'm sorry," Gracie murmured.

She wasn't sorry though, not really. How could she be? She was just being polite, just saying what people were supposed to in these situations.

"Don't be," Abs assured her. "By the time he went, he wasn't really my dad anymore. I don't think he had been for a long time. He just sort of…looked like him."

Gracie thought about that for a moment, staring down at the laundry bag she'd tossed aside. The one that was forever tainted with the smell of stale alcohol. "I don't really think my dad is my dad anymore either."

"You don't?"

"No. He's not like other people's dads. He doesn't ask me about how school went, or help me with my homework, or talk to me about my friends. He cares when I get a bad report card, but I think that's because it makes *him* look bad. I mean, he knows I'm failing math class, but he never actually cares until a teacher calls home about it."

It was the most Abs had ever heard Gracie say before. The words came out in a jumbled mess, tumbling out of Gracie's mouth like one long stream of consciousness.

She paused for a breath after finishing, inhaling deeply. "Sorry."

"Don't apologize. I get it. It's nice to be able to talk to someone about all this, especially if you've been holding it in all this time."

Gracie exhaled shakily, tearing her gaze from the laundry bag to look up at Abs. "I don't talk to anyone about any of this stuff. I tried talking to all my friends, but they just...don't get it."

Abs winced at that. It was exactly the same experience she'd had to suffer through during her own teenage years. At first, she'd tried talking to her friends about her dad, but they'd all just laughed it off and said something about their own dad liking beer a little too much. Everyone treated it as though it was no big deal until it was too late.

"They all just think he's like other dads. They think that everyone drinks, and I'm making a big deal out of it."

"You're not," Abs assured her.

"I know I'm not!" Gracie huffed out a bitter sigh. She looked down at the filthy laundry room floor with a heavy sigh, folding her arms over her chest, and pouting a little.

It was overwhelming, being in that position. Barely being a teenager, and looking at the rest of your life as it stretched out in front of you, with an ever-debilitating alcoholic as a role model to look up to—it was rough. Abs remembered that feeling well. She remembered feeling *different* and isolated, while she listened to all her friends talking about their dads. At the very least, she could impart some wisdom on the kid.

"Do you want to know my secret?" Abs asked. "To surviving life with someone like that?" She jerked her thumb in the direction of the door to the stairwell, as if Ed was standing right there.

"How?"

"You've got to have a *thing*. A hobby, or an interest. Something that you're passionate about, something that you love. But something that he can't touch. It gives you something to escape into when it gets too much. An outlet, or a distraction. If you let him touch every part of your life, then it'll end up consuming you."

Gracie nodded slowly, but the frown was still there. "I mean, he doesn't care about anything to do with me, anyway."

"Yeah, but this is different. This is something that you have complete control over, something that's completely yours. Something you don't feel like you have to share with him, the way you do with school."

"What was your thing?" Gracie asked. "Your private thing that he didn't know about?"

"Boxing." Abs grinned.

"Figures. You've got shoulders like a linebacker."

Abs laughed at that. "I ought to, after all the time I've booked in at the gym."

For a moment, the two fell silent, just listening to the low hum of their machines. It wasn't like the silence the first time they had met, though. It wasn't heavy and suffocating, pressing down on them and leaving a lingering sense of anxiety in its wake. It was easy, calm, almost relaxing.

"You know," Abs said finally, looking over at the teenager. "If you're looking for something to do, or even just a place to go after school when you want to get out of the house, I work at Sapphy's Gym on East 1st. You can always just sit in my office for a couple of hours if you don't want to be here."

Gracie shifted on the spot, looking a little uncomfortable. "I don't really...have the money for a class."

"I'm sure we can figure something out," Abs assured her, patting her on the shoulder. "The invitation is there if you want to take me up on it."

"Thanks." Gracie looked up at Abs and smiled.

21

It wasn't the tight-lipped, uncomfortable smile of someone who was just trying to be polite. It was a genuinely warm smile, a smile of relief that *finally* someone had seen what was going on. Not only that, but someone really understood what she was going through.

Abs paused before speaking again. "I saw your dad leaving on my way out."

Gracie's lip curled. She turned her head away. "Yeah. He's got a *date*."

"A date?"

"Some girl he met on Tinder. That's what he spends most of his time doing when he's not at work—I see him just scrolling through all their pictures, choosing the ones he likes. And I saw some messages he was sending them. They were gross."

Poor kid.

This wasn't a childhood, doing her father's laundry for him while he was out on dates. She should have been stressing over homework and staying up too late calling her friends instead of…doing this. It wasn't fair.

"You got plans for dinner? My mom always makes too much."

"Nah." She shrugged. "I've got pizza. Dad left me some money for takeout, but I picked up a cheap frozen pizza when I came back from school, so I'm going to save the money."

"You sure?" Abs asked with a frown. "You don't want a nice home cooked meal? It's pasta."

"Nope." Gracie smiled at her, and again, it was a genuine smile. It lit up her eyes and instantly brightened her round face. "Don't worry about me. But thanks."

That was easier said than done. Abs hopped off the dryer and said goodbye to Gracie, before heading up to her mom's apartment, and even when she sat down to eat with her mom, the girl was on her mind. Normally, she'd end up taking some leftovers home with her, but as she headed for the door with her Tupperware in hand, she stopped.

22

"Mom?" She pushed the container back into her mother's hands. "Do me a favor? The next time you see Gracie, can you give her this instead?"

"The girl from next door?"

"I'm pretty sure she's living on a diet of takeout and convenience store microwave meals," Abs admitted, frowning. "I just…would feel a little more comfortable if I knew she was getting fed, you know?"

Maria smiled down at her daughter, reaching out to stroke a short strand of blonde hair out of her eyes. "That's very sweet of you."

"It's not *that* sweet." Abs laughed. "Anyway, I'm going home. Don't let the kid starve, and I'll be back tomorrow."

She let the door to her mom's apartment close behind her and for a few moments, she just stood there in the hallway, trying to listen out for any noise coming from Gracie's apartment. There was nothing, no voices or television, so she headed downstairs and walked out to her car.

Poor *kid.*

Four

A few days passed after Abs extended the offer to Gracie to train at the gym with her, but there was no sign of her. Abs didn't run into her in the hallways of her mom's building either, so she didn't get the chance to ask if she'd given the classes any more thought. A week went by, and Abs just figured Gracie had decided against it.

It was about midway into her late shift when Gracie appeared. Abs wasn't teaching that evening, but because a couple of the younger girls who went to the gym had upcoming matches, she was keeping a watchful eye on them. She knew that some younger fighters who worked out at the gym had a real problem of slacking off right before a fight. Hell, at one point she'd done the same thing—it was easy enough to have that arrogant 'I'm untouchable' attitude after a few wins.

Someone needed to watch them, especially if they were there without their trainers. Someone needed to pick up on their sloppy footwork and stupid mistakes. Tonight, that someone was her.

"Hey, Abs." Logan poked her head through the door that led to the lobby. "There's a kid out here who says she's looking for you."

"A kid?"

"Well, a teenager."

For a moment, Abs was a little confused. She didn't normally get visitors at work, and she didn't even *know* any teenagers outside the gym, so who would it be—Wait. She did know one.

Gracie.

Leaving her position at the corner of the room, Abs followed Logan out to the lobby where, sure enough, Gracie was waiting for her.

"So you decided to come along," Abs said with a small smile. Gracie nodded, looking around the lobby. She didn't seem too impressed.

"Yeah," she murmured. "You made it sound like this place was some super high-tech gym. I thought it was abandoned when I walked past."

Behind Gracie, at the front desk, Abs saw Logan look up sharply and glare at the girl. Abs bit back her smile and turned her attention back to the surprisingly surly teen.

"Don't judge it too quickly. Did you bring something to wear?"

Gracie motioned to her backpack, which was slung over one shoulder. "My gym kit for school."

"Good. The changing rooms are over there." Abs pointed to the hallway on their left. "It's right at the end. Go get changed and meet me inside."

Gracie disappeared down the hallway, leaving Abs and Logan staring at each other.

"Charming kid," Logan said finally.

"Yeah." Abs grinned. "She's kind of an asshole."

"Perfect for you, then."

"Yeah, yeah." She rolled her eyes, chuckling. "I'm going back in."

It didn't take Gracie long to follow her back out, practically bouncing on her toes as she ran over to join Abs.

"Okay, so where do I start?" she asked with a grin. "When do I get to start fighting?"

"Easy, Rambo." Abs laughed. The enthusiasm was encouraging, but Gracie had a long way to go before she was going to be allowed in the ring. "You've got a few things you need to learn first."

"Learn?" Gracie echoed with a groan. "Come on, just give me some gloves and let—"

She broke off, punching the air in front of her, hunching into what she must have thought was a boxer's stance. Abs chuckled, shaking her head.

Yeah, the kid had a long way to go.

"Well, for starters, this isn't just about how hard or fast you can hit your opponent. There's a lot more to it than that."

"Right…" Gracie said, clearly not convinced.

Abs didn't exactly blame her though; she'd felt the same way when she'd first started boxing. "It's more like…art, in a way. It's a dance between you and your opponent. You can't just blindly use your fists without thinking. You've always got to be planning three steps ahead and thinking about what the other person might be doing next. That's how you win."

"So, it's like…chess?"

"Exactly! Like chess!"

Gracie looked over at the ring where two girls were sparring. It was only a practice round, with light jabs and no knockouts, but to someone like Gracie with no experience, it probably looked real.

"Come here." Abs beckoned her over to the ringside so they could watch the match together. "Watch them for a moment, but don't focus on the fists. Everyone always focuses on the fists, but I want you to look at their bodies—the way they hold themselves, the way they move."

"What's so important about that?"

"It's the foundation, the base. How can you expect to throw a half decent punch if you're standing wrong?"

Gracie looked down at her feet, shuffling them on the mat. "What's wrong with the way I stand?"

"Get back into a fighter's stance, the way you did before."

Gracie did as she was told, dropping her knees a little and swaying from side to side. She tucked her chin towards her chest, bringing her fists up close to her face. It wasn't a bad start, especially since she probably had no idea what she was doing.

"Okay, that's pretty good. Let's start from the top and work down. You're keeping your head tucked in, which is

26

good. It'll mean your throat is protected, which you'll want. Your shoulders though..."

Abs leaned over and placed her hands on Gracie's shoulders, pushing down on them. "Relax them. They're too hunched up. When you box, you want to strike a balance between being tensed up enough that you can throw a solid punch, and relaxed enough that you can still dodge and move around."

They moved on, with Abs pointing out the little details of Gracie's posture that she wouldn't have known needed correcting. She needed to relax her shoulders and knees, but keep her stomach pulled in taut. Getting hit in a relaxed stomach was a good way to do some real damage to your internal organs.

"Okay." She smiled at Gracie. "You want to get started for real?"

She led Gracie over to the punching bags at the far end of the room, away from the prying eyes of more seasoned boxers. The last thing Gracie needed on day one was the stress of being watched by other people.

Before she set Gracie up with another fighter, Abs needed to make sure she had the basics down. Planning, intuition, precision—all of that would come later. Before any of that though, Gracie needed to learn how to throw a punch, and she needed to know how to dodge a punch.

They spent time working the bag, mainly so that Gracie could get a feel for the resistance and weight of it. Abs was impressed. The kid had some speed to her, and when she struck out at the bag, she seemed to be able to hit out at pretty much the same spot over and over.

"This is a good start." She grinned. Gracie stopped hitting the bag and leaned into it instead, sweat already beading on her forehead. "Now, let's get you moving."

"Moving?" Gracie echoed, her voice already rushed and breathless.

"Bend your knees a little, but remember not to lock them. Then, start to move from side to side. You're trying to make yourself as hard to hit as possible. So when you move, try not to follow a pattern, because your opponent will be able to see that, and they'll figure out how and when to hit you."

"Okay," Gracie murmured, a little uncertain. She stretched up on her toes and began to dance from side to side in front of the bag.

"That's it, just like that." Abs grinned, watching Gracie move around.

She seemed to be picking things up quickly. Far more quickly than some other girls Abs had helped. More than once, Abs had struggled to make the very simple point about keeping on your toes, which only a few newbies understood when they first arrived. Some of them had so little experience before walking in there that Abs often found she had to spend the entire first training session just working on posture.

Gracie, on the other hand, seemed to have a natural talent. Maybe it was because she felt that same spark, the same rush of energy that Abs had done all those years earlier when she had first started training. Or, more likely, maybe she just liked the catharsis of laying punches into a bag over and over again.

There was a lot more to training than just working the bag, and Abs knew that. There were drills that tested cardio and endurance; burpees and wind sprints from one end of the hall to the other; exercises that perfected her footwork; conditioning her to keep moving and dance around her opponent. All of that could come later though; she didn't want to overload Gracie on her first day at the gym. Instead, she just worked out all her pent up energy and frustration.

It didn't take long for Abs to see the *look* in Gracie's eyes. It was the same expression that most people in the gym had on their faces at one point or another—the look of a person who was focused and fixated on one thing, to the point where the rest of the world was just white noise. Abs herself had worn that same expression many times before over the years, and it was interesting to see that change come over her so suddenly.

Even Logan was impressed. She dipped in and out of the hall, checking up on some other clients who were hard at work. From across the hall, she shot Abs a quick thumbs up when she saw how hard Gracie was working. Flyaway wisps of dark hair stuck to her forehead, slicked against her skin with sweat, and her skin was flushed red. By the time Abs checked the time on her phone, ready to call it a night, the girl looked exhausted.

"Alright," Abs said with a smile, holding her hand up to Gracie. "I think it's time we called it quits, don't you?"

"Definitely." Gracie huffed between pants. "I'm ready to go home."

Abs chuckled and tossed her a bottle of water from the vending machine in the lobby. "Sip that, don't gulp it. Why don't you go have a quick shower, and then I'll drive you home?"

"Fine by me." Gracie pulled off her gloves with an exhausted grin and tossed them to Abs before heading off towards the main doors. Abs watched her go with a small smile, then headed to the equipment locker room to pack away the gloves.

Logan was back behind the desk talking to her girlfriend, Dani, when she came out. "Saw that kid heading to the showers. You training her up for boot camp or something? She looked like a wreck." Logan chuckled.

"Hi Dani." Abs nodded to the dark-haired woman before answering Logan. "No, nothing like that. I was just showing her the ropes. It was her first session, so I figured she could just tire herself out at the bag for tonight."

"It's not like you to get all maternal like this," Logan pointed out.

"I wouldn't call it maternal. More like – I don't know – big-sisterly. I'm just looking out for her."

"Hmm." Logan nodded slowly, cocking her head to one side. "Where did you find her, anyway?"

Abs explained the story of how she'd met Gracie. Well, she explained *parts* of the story of how she met Gracie. She told Logan and Dani about meeting her in the laundry room of her mom's building, told her about *most* of their conversation, but she skirted around the details. She left out the alcoholic father and left out the air of misery that had hung around Gracie the first time they'd met. That wasn't her story to tell.

Gracie didn't take long in the shower, and when she was ready, Abs said goodbye to Logan and Dani, and walked Gracie out to the car. The two got in, and she let Gracie fiddle around with the radio until she found a station she liked.

"So what do you think of boxing? Did you enjoy it?"

"Yeah, I did." Gracie grinned. "I'm tired, though. Hungry, too. Can we stop in at a 7-11 on the way home?"

"A 7-11?" Abs echoed. "What? No way."

"Why not?"

"Because part of training involves you eating right. You're eating with me tonight; a proper home-cooked meal. Okay?"

"Okay," Gracie said quietly, looking down at her hands. "Thank you."

Abs glanced at the girl out of the corner of her eye, frowning. *When was the last time she'd had a home cooked meal?* She suspected Ed wasn't much of a chef, given that his idea of feeding her was to leave money for takeout.

"So how did you start doing this? Boxing, I mean," Gracie asked finally. "Did you have a neighbor with daddy issues too?"

Abs laughed at that, shaking her head. "No. I was always a pretty sporty kid, and when things started to get really bad with my dad, I ended up signing onto a whole load of after-school sports groups, just so I'd have an excuse to not go home. My school had a pretty good gym facility and had some punching bags. At first, it was just a good way to get out some of that frustration I had, but then a teacher suggested I take some classes and...well, I really liked it, and I was good, too."

"How good?"

"Well, I got into college on a sports scholarship, so I reckon I was pretty good." Abs grinned. "And my fighting record was pretty impressive, if I say so myself."

"Wait, you fought?" Gracie asked. "Like—actually fought? Like what's on TV?"

"Women's boxing still doesn't get all that much recognition, but yeah. I fought."

"If you were so good, then how come you stopped?"

"I got into a car accident," Abs explained. "On my way back from a fight, actually. My right hand was crushed, and I had to have metal pins put in to support the bones."

"For real?" Gracie peered over at her hand, which rested on the top of the steering wheel. "Cool! Do you have a scar?"

"Two, actually." As they pulled up to a red light, Abs flicked on the overhead light and held out her hand to Gracie so she could see the scars that ran along the bones of her forefinger and thumb. Gracie grabbed her hand to look more closely.

"Cool," she repeated, grinning. "But does it hurt?"

"Sometimes," Abs admitted.

"Is that why you don't fight any more?"

"Hmm." Abs flicked off the overhead light as she rested her hand on the steering wheel again. "It's too painful. I can't train for as long as I would need to because it hurts too much, and if I was to go up against someone in the ring, I know I'd be in agony. I don't think I'd ever be able to win a match with my hand like this."

Gracie frowned, looking up at her. "Do you miss it? Fighting?"

Abs hadn't actually thought about fighting in a long time. It was a secret part of her mind she'd locked away, and she never allowed herself to dwell on it. She didn't let herself think about the adrenaline rush right after a match, or the sound of people cheering her on from the sides. But when she thought about it now, yes. She missed it.

"I do," she admitted with a small, sad smile. "It was a big part of my life for a long time, and I think I felt a little empty without it, you know?"

The memory of those first few months of recovery were still bitter. It still hurt, a little, to remember what it had felt like the first time she'd looked down at her bandaged hand after getting out of surgery. But it wasn't all bad. Some good had come out of it, at least. She wouldn't have her job at the gym, and she probably wouldn't be around for her mom as much if she was still fighting.

But she did still miss the competition.

When they arrived back at the apartment building, the offer of a home-cooked meal was too much for Gracie to resist, and so she eagerly sat down to eat with Abs and Maria, even going in for seconds when her plate was cleared. She told Maria all about her first class at the gym, dropping in a few complaints here and there about how hard Abs had worked her, while grinning across the table at them.

She didn't stop smiling through the whole meal, Abs realized. And it wasn't the wry smile that she'd seen before, the one that was far too old for Gracie's young face. It was a genuine, toothy grin that lit up her whole face, threatening to split it in two as she went on and on about the new moves she'd learned.

For the first time since Abs had met her, Gracie looked like a kid. She didn't look like the 'good kid' dutifully hauling laundry down to the basement, or tossing out garbage in the black alley. She looked like any other regular thirteen-year-old kid, and it was nice.

Even if it was just for an evening.

32

Five

Over the next couple of weeks, Gracie began spending more and more time at the gym. She would usually show up after school, spend some time working with Abs or on her own, and then she would wait for Abs in her office, and get a ride home. Sometimes, Abs would pop her head into her office to check on how Gracie was doing, and she'd see her with a book on her lap, studying. Hopefully, it was for math.

Those quiet stolen hours in Abs's office were probably a much nicer place to study for school than Ed's place, where she'd have to listen to her father getting progressively more and more drunk. Abs was more than happy to sacrifice her office space to the teenager for a little while, if it meant she could help in any way. She always offered to help with homework too, (just as long as it wasn't math), but there wasn't much she could do.

Gracie was making real progress in the gym, too. When she'd first started with Abs, she had been plenty eager, but she'd had no technical skill whatsoever. Over the past couple of weeks though, that had changed. She was faster now, her movements were more precise. She had some natural talent there, which gave them a lot to work with, but she was actually willing to put in the effort to improve as well. Abs was proud of all the growth she'd shown in the gym.

And then Gracie just stopped showing up.

She stopped appearing in the doorway, waving at Abs from across the hall. She stopped hovering around Abs's office, and she stopped hitching rides home.

No one else really seemed that concerned, and they just seemed to brush it off as nothing more than Gracie getting bored. She was a teenager, after all. Teenagers were flaky; they got bored quickly; they found new hobbies, new interests. And hey, it wasn't like she had any kind of obligation to show up to the classes with Abs. Maybe she was studying for an exam and didn't have time to come to the gym. Maybe she was sick and taking some time to recover.

But still, Abs was worried.

With every day where there was no sign of Gracie, Abs worried more. And what was worse, she couldn't see any sign of Gracie when she went to visit her mom, either. She didn't see her coming home with groceries, or doing the laundry, or taking out the trash. She'd knocked on the door to the apartment a couple times, but there had been no answer.

Almost a week passed with no sign of Gracie, and Abs was at her mom's place, doing a load of laundry for her. Again though, just like every other day that she'd looked out for the teenager, she couldn't see her.

Abs was heading back upstairs with the freshly dried clothes, when she ran into Ed on the stairwell. He didn't look as good as he had done the last time they'd met. His hair was greasy and unkempt; he was several days out from his last shave, and he was dressed in sweatpants and a stained t-shirt.

Ed peered at her in the gloom of the stairwell, before his eyes widened in recognition. He smiled at her—the same broad, strangely cold smile she'd seen from him before. "Ah! Jen! It's good to see you again."

He was drunk. He was talking too loudly, being too friendly with her, and he was swaying on the staircase. As Abs took another step up, she could smell the booze on his breath. It was mid afternoon, so when had he started drinking?

"Hi, Ed," she said quietly, pulling back just enough that she was out of range of his breath. God, that smell was repulsive. She'd hated it when she was thirteen, and she hated it now.

"You doing good?" he asked, flashing that smile again.

"I'm fine. You?"

"Oh," he sighed before shrugging at her. "Good. Can't complain, you know?"

"Yeah." Abs shot him a tight-lipped smile, but just like the last time they'd spoken, he either couldn't tell that she wasn't interested in talking to him, or he didn't care. "How's Gracie? I haven't seen her around in a while?"

Then, just like that, his demeanor changed. It was eerie, seeing the shift in his expression; he went from friendly and open to...cold. There was no other way to describe it. His expression was sullen, and as he leaned back against the banister to support himself, he let out a low sigh.

"Oh. Gracie..." He nodded slowly. "She moved out."

She moved out? She was a thirteen-year-old kid. There was no way she'd just wandered out on her own. Did he really expect her to just believe that?

"She moved out?" Abs echoed, cocking an eyebrow. "When? Why?"

"Living with Hayley, her mom," he grunted.

Well, at least that was something. At least if she was living with her mom, she was somewhere safe, and away from him.

Abs excused herself and sidestepped Ed before walking up to her mom's apartment. As she climbed the stairs, she heard his heavy footsteps below her. Even the sound of him shuffling around on the stairwell, falling onto the banister in an attempt to keep himself upright, was enough to make her shudder. That sound was all too familiar to her.

Thankfully, the sound of Ed's stumbling, drunken footsteps faded as he made it to the ground floor, and by the time Abs made it into her mom's apartment, she couldn't hear   him   at   all.

Six

Almost two weeks of total radio silence had passed before Gracie showed up in the gym again as if nothing had happened. Abs was in her office when she arrived, but Logan sent her upstairs. She walked in without bothering to knock.

"Hey," she called out, grinning at Abs. Her school bag was slung over one shoulder, just like always, and she was dressed in her gym kit. "You busy?"

"Gracie!" Abs leapt up from behind her desk, staring at her. "Where have you been?! I haven't seen you in weeks! Your dad told me you'd moved out, and I didn't have any way to contact you."

"Moved out?" Gracie echoed, rolling her eyes. "Yeah. Sure, I moved out, after he tossed me out."

She let her bag slide from her shoulder and hit the floor, before throwing herself down into the chair across from Abs's.

"Are you okay?" Abs asked gently. Gracie shrugged nonchalantly, picking at her nails for a moment. She certainly didn't *look* bothered.

"Yeah, I'm fine," she said, with the same note of denial that Abs recognized from her own teenage years. It was one of those lies that you started to believe once you'd said it enough times. "I'm living back with my mom again."

Good. She hadn't said much about her mom, other than her working in emergency dispatch and had to pull some crappy shifts. Abs didn't know much about the woman, but she figured that pretty much anything was better than living alone with Ed.

"Do you want to talk about it?" she asked, a little hesitant. She knew this would be sensitive territory for Gracie, and she had to tread lightly.

36

"Not really," she admitted, shrugging again. "I'm fine. I like living with my mom, even though she's kind of—on my case a lot."

"On your case?"

"You know, she's checking up on me all the time, always poking her head into my room and coming in to try to talk to me. I dunno, it's weird."

"Kind of sounds like she's missed having you around," Abs pointed out.

It couldn't have been an easy decision for her mother to make, leaving her daughter alone with a man she knew could never be a reliable father. It was only natural she was trying to make up for that time they'd spent apart.

"Yeah. I guess so." Gracie stretched out languidly in the chair. "So, are you busy?"

Abs thought about saying yes. She thought about sitting Gracie down and having a serious conversation, explaining that she couldn't keep drifting through all this shit and act like it was nothing. Sooner or later, that attitude was going to bite her on the ass, and she was going to regret it.

But she wasn't her parent, and it wasn't her job. What mattered right now was that Gracie wasn't living with Ed anymore, and beyond that, this wasn't really Abs's concern. So instead of leaning over the desk with her fingers interlaced and trying to talk to Gracie about her feelings, Abs just smiled.

"Go get warmed up downstairs," she told Gracie. "I'll be down there in a moment."

Gracie left her bag on the floor and rushed downstairs to get started on her first workout. As she watched the teenager run off, Abs couldn't help but laugh to herself. It was good to see that she was still eager.

The first workout went better than she had expected. After two weeks off, Gracie was a little rusty, but she hadn't forgotten the few core things that Abs had drilled into her. She kept her chin tucked in, her shoulders relaxed, her stomach pulled in tight. She stayed on her toes when she fought, moving around the bag as she struck out at it over and over again.

Just like every other time she'd come to the gym, Abs dropped Gracie off home after class. As it turned out, her mom's place was on the way back to Abs's own apartment, so it wasn't like she had to go miles out of her way to make sure the kid got home safe.

"So, what does your mom think of this? Is she happy you've got a hobby?" Abs asked, as they pulled into Gracie's street. The light was out at the house they stopped by, and it didn't look like anyone was home. Maybe her mom was at work.

"Uh? She's cool with it, thinks it's great," Gracie said quickly, unbuckling her seatbelt. She opened the door without looking at Abs properly. "I'll uh, see you later, bye!"

With that, she hopped out of the car before Abs could say another word, and rushed out to the front door. Abs waited until one of the downstairs lights flicked on, and then she put the car back into gear and headed off.

She was glad that Gracie had decided to come to classes after all. This was something that could really help her the same way it had helped Abs, and the fact that she wasn't living with her father anymore was comforting. Of course, it wasn't like Abs knew nothing about Gracie's mom except that she worked long hours, but she couldn't be much worse than Ed.

* * *

Abs met Hayley, Gracie's mom, for the first time during Gracie's next session.

Gracie came back to the gym just like she always did a couple of days later, ready for another workout. It seemed like she was happy to settle back into the little routine the two of them had started before she'd been kicked out of her dad's place, and Abs was glad to have her back. It was nice to look over the main floor of the gym and see her working on one of the bags, lost in her own little world.

They were halfway through class, working with skipping ropes to try to improve Gracie's footwork, when this blonde ball of fury showed up out of the blue. It was a pretty quiet evening, with only a few people milling around. There were a couple of people in the far corner with the speed bags; Logan was working with Dana, a young girl who had her first match coming up in a few weeks, and Abs was keeping Gracie on her toes with the ropes.

Abs back was to the door, so when Hayley came into the main hall of the gym, Abs didn't even notice her at first. It wasn't until Gracie caught sight of her mother at the far end of the room and stopped in her tracks that Abs turned.

Abs didn't recognize the woman. She was maybe a little older than Abs and she wasn't dressed in sports gear, so she wasn't here to work out. One thing was for sure, though. The woman was on a mission. At first, Abs didn't even notice the resemblance between this new woman and the teenager beside her, until Gracie swore under her breath.

"Oh shit!"

"Oh shit *what*?" Abs asked. Before Gracie could answer, the woman spotted them and crossed the room, heading in their direction.

"Abby!" she called out loudly. "What the hell are you *doing* here?"

"Hey, Mom," Gracie said quietly. The skipping rope in her hands dropped to her side, and she managed a sheepish smile for her mother. "I didn't think you'd be back from work yet."

"You want to explain to me why I came home to an empty home and a note on the refrigerator? I was out of my *mind* when I couldn't find you. I nearly sent out half the neighborhood looking for you!"

This was Gracie's mom?

"I left a note," Gracie protested weakly, unable to meet her mom's gaze.

"A *note*. Not a text, not a voicemail. A *note*. Why am I paying for your phone if you're not going to tell me where you are?"

So much for *'she knows I'm here, and she's cool with it'*, Abs thought bitterly, shaking her head. Beside her, Gracie was shifting from foot to foot. She'd fucked up, and she knew it.

"What am I supposed to do, track your phone when I'm not home so I know where you are? Is that what you'd like?"

She was upset, and angry too. And to be fair, she had every right to be. Abs couldn't imagine how furious she'd have been to come home and find her own child missing, but at the same time, yelling at Gracie in the middle of a hall of people wasn't going to solve anything.

The yelling wasn't just embarrassing and frustrating for Gracie, but it was starting to disrupt everyone who was around them as well. Logan had stopped to look over at them. Abs knew that she wouldn't step in unless she was needed, but it was good to see her in her peripheral vision, leaning on the ropes.

In an attempt to try to diffuse the situation and calm Hayley down so that they could all actually talk to each other, Abs decided to step in.

"Hi there, excuse me?" She waved her hands to get their attention. "You must be Gracie's mom. It's Hayley, isn't it?"

Hayley turned her fiery gaze on Abs. "And who are you?"

On instinct, Abs switched on her customer service voice. It was the one she had perfected while working part time at the local grocery store in high school, and it had been very useful on more than one occasion since she had started working at the gym. "I'm one of the trainers here, Abs. I'm also the assistant manager, so—"

"So *what*?" Hayley snapped, folding her arms over her chest. "Is that supposed to give you some credibility?"

Well, yeah, Abs thought. That was sort of the point. But as much as she wanted to say that, she bit her tongue and kept quiet. Pissing Hayley off wouldn't exactly be a smart move.

"Do you *normally* allow thirteen-year-old children to sneak off so they can learn how to fight?" Hayley continued. Her voice wasn't raised anymore, she wasn't borderline shouting at Abs, but now she was speaking with that note of frosty disappointment that only a parent really knew how to wield. "Is that a policy at this gym that I'm unaware of?"

"Well, I *thought* Gracie had your permission to be here," Abs explained, shooting Gracie a dark look. To her credit, she did look a little ashamed about how all of this had turned out, and bowed her head.

"Based on what?" Hayley laughed, shaking her head in disbelief. "Her word? Are you *that* naïve? Or are you just stupid?"

Jesus, Lady, Abs thought bitterly. *It's not my fault your kid doesn't tell you stuff.*

The insult stung a little, but Abs swallowed whatever petty retort was on the tip of her tongue. Shooting back some bitchy comment was probably the worst thing to do, and she knew it. Instead, she took a deep breath in, steadied herself, and tried to reply as calmly as possible.

"I understand that you're upset with me, and with Gracie. But I can promise you that Gracie was never in any harm while she was here with us."

Hayley snorted at that. "You expect me to believe that?"

41

What exactly did this woman think was going on here? Did she think they were passing out free crack at the door or something?

"Gracie has been completely safe here. All of our staff have had their full background checks done, and we've got CCTV cameras everywhere so that—"

"You're teaching her how to *fight*! I mean, look at this place!" Hayley gestured around the room, at the exercise machines and weights, at the punching bags lined up against the wall, then at the ring, which was still occupied by Logan and the kid she was training. All things that Abs saw most days of the week. All just regular, normal facets of a gym.

But the pieces *finally* fell into place for Abs as Hayley said that. She stopped in her tracks as she realized that Hayley's problem – or at the very least, her *biggest* problem – wasn't the fact that this was a room full of strangers who were looking after her daughter. Her problem was the boxing itself.

"You—you don't like the fact that I'm teaching Gracie how to box?" she said slowly.

"God, of course I don't! What kind of mother would? I mean, look! I don't want my daughter in the ring with—with someone like that!" Hayley gestured towards the ring where Logan was still leaning on the ropes, watching the scene unfold with a grin. At least *someone* was enjoying this, because Abs sure as shit wasn't.

Logan held up a gloved hand and waved at them and as she did, Abs's facade of professionalism slipped. "Well shit, Logan's a gold medalist in her weight class. *I* wouldn't want Gracie in there with her either. I'd never put her up against a rookie."

By this time though, Hayley's outrage had drawn the attention of most of the other people in the gym, even those who normally had their headphones on so they could focus on their workout. They were all craning their necks, looking over curiously, all while trying *not* to look like they were too

42

interested in what was going on. Abs knew that if she kept arguing out here in the open, she'd be the one to get yelled at about it when Sapphy found out, so in an attempt to mediate the situation, she looked over at Gracie, who was watching from the sidelines.

"Gracie, why don't you go and get changed out of your gym gear. I'm going to talk to your mom for a bit."

Gracie opened her mouth to protest, but when Hayley shot her a pointed look, she closed it again and sloped off towards the lobby doors with a scowl. The two women watched her leave, and when the door swung shut behind her, Abs turned back to Hayley.

"Shall we talk?" she offered, gesturing to the side door that led up towards her office. Hayley pursed her lips disapprovingly, but agreed to follow Abs up with a terse nod.

Abs let the two of them into her office, offering Hayley a seat in front of the desk as she dropped into her own one. "You know Gracie isn't in any danger here, right? All of our trainers are either currently competing, or are former competitors, and most of us started when we were about Gracie's age."

She'd talked to quite a few worried parents through their kid's first session at the gym. She'd soothed their worries from the sidelines while their kid enjoyed learning the ropes, and normally by the end of the conversation, they'd seem comfortable enough to sign their daughter up for classes.

But with Hayley, she could tell things were going to be different.

"I don't like the idea of Gracie learning to fight." She began twisting her hands together in her lap. "I don't want her thinking that this kind of violence is okay. Especially not with the way things are right now. She's already acting out, getting kicked out of class and failing math. The last thing I need is someone encouraging her to fight on top of all that."

Abs took a deep breath in, rocking backwards in her chair slowly. She'd had this conversation so many times over the years before she'd even begun working at the gym. Even back when she'd taken up boxing in high school, she'd still have to deal with other girls in gym class calling her a freak or a bully, a girl who was just looking for an excuse to hit something. She'd heard those same sentiments from parents too, but they were just packaged a little differently.

But Hayley was different. She was...determined. Belligerent, even. And it was taking all of Abs's self control not to let her professional facade slip again.

"Do you really think I'm teaching Gracie how to be a thug or something?"

"I think she doesn't need anyone glorifying beating another person into a pulp."

Abs leaned back in her chair, breathing through her nose as she looked at the woman. She had no history or experience at all with boxing, other than perhaps catching a few glimpses of the knockouts on TV. It was to be expected that she was reacting like this—people were scared of what they didn't fully understand. She was behaving like this out of love for her daughter, that much was obvious. And despite the fact that Abs thought she was being naïve, she had to admire that at least. She could hardly fault a mother for wanting to do everything she could to protect her child.

But she was going about it the wrong way.

"You want a word of advice, from one former troubled kid to the mother of a currently troubled kid?" Abs offered, keeping her voice low and gentle. She didn't want this offer of help to seem like she was attacking Hayley's parenting skills in any way, after all.

She didn't bother waiting for Hayley to respond before she offered the advice up, anyway. "I think Gracie needs this. She gets discipline out of the training, a sense of pride and achievement. At the very least, it's a good workout for her. And if you're worried about the fee, I've already told Gracie I'll waive the cost of classes, so you won't have to—"

"I'm not worried about the fee," Hayley snapped, her face curling into a scowl as she folded her arms over her chest.

Abs didn't want to give in. She didn't want to just step aside and let Gracie leave here with her mother. She *knew* that this was a good opportunity for the girl, just like it had been for her when she was in the same situation. Worst of all, she knew Hayley was dismissing this far too quickly.

But what could she do, really? When push came to shove, this was Hayley's choice, and she had to respect that.

"Boxing is about a lot more than just hitting the other person," Abs said slowly. "And I'd appreciate it if you took the time to learn that, like Gracie is doing. But at the end of the day, I can't force you to like this. And Gracie is a minor, so this is your call. So if you really don't want her to have classes here anymore, she won't have classes here anymore."

"That's what I want," Hayley said sharply, nodding.

And that was it. That was the end of the matter. Abs just sighed, motioning towards the door. "I'd recommend you help Gracie find something else instead. Maybe some other kind of sport."

"I don't need your help to raise my daughter," Hayley said coldly, standing up and pulling her jacket around herself a little more. "Goodnight."

Without waiting for a response, she turned on her heel and left Abs's office, letting the door slam shut behind her on her way out. Abs winced at the noise, before swinging around in her chair to look out of the window at the main floor below. When she peered down, she could see Hayley marching across the room towards the lobby, her long brown hair swinging in its ponytail.

Abs only got a few moments of peace before the door opened again, and she turned to see Logan walking over.

"You alright?" she asked.

Abs just shrugged. She was disappointed, but there was nothing more she could have done. She tried to make her case to Hayley, but it had fallen on deaf ears.

"Well, at least we know where Gracie gets her charming personality from." Logan flopped down in the chair Hayley had just vacated, sighing heavily. "Her mom's a real peach."

"She's not so bad," Abs admitted, rocking backwards in her chair.

"She thinks we're teaching her kid Mortal Kombat moves in here."

Abs laughed at that, staring up at the ceiling. Sure, Hayley had been in no mood to hear any arguments about why Gracie should keep training, but her heart had been in the right place.

"She's just worried about her daughter, the same as any parent."

"She doesn't need to take it out on us. It's just as well Sapphy wasn't in." Logan nodded towards Sapphy's office. "Sapphy would have torn strips off her. You're too nice."

"I don't know, I liked it," Abs admitted with a grin, looking over at Logan. "I like women with a bit of a bite to them."

"You're a sadist."

"Technically, that'd make me a masochist." Abs flexed her hand, wincing as she curled her fingers into a fist. Her hand was starting to hurt again, not bad, just a twinge, but enough that she noticed it. "But I see your point."

"Hmm." Logan stood up, pointing to Abs's hand. "Seriously, get that checked out."

"Yeah, thank you." Abs rolled her eyes. "Time for you to go."

Logan did as she was told, leaving Abs alone in her office, with the faint ache in her fingers for company as she thought about Hayley. She hadn't had a particularly strong image of Gracie's mom built up in her mind's eye. Gracie hadn't talked much about her mom, so she had very little to go on, but whatever she'd imagined Hayley to be like, it didn't come close to the reality.

Abs had thought she'd have been quieter, maybe a little meeker. She certainly hadn't expected her to burst in like some furious avenging angel, with her hair flying about, ready to pluck her daughter out of the ring. Abs knew she probably should have felt a little more embarrassed about getting yelled at in front of fellow trainers and clients alike, but for some reason, she didn't. If anything, she had a little begrudging respect for the woman—it took some balls to waltz into a building as if she was the fountain of all knowledge and act as though she knew better than everyone else. And she was pretty, too. That wasn't really the point, but in Abs's mind, it was a bonus.

But at the end of the day, that wasn't what was important. What *was* important was that Hayley had pulled Gracie out of her classes. Abs knew it wasn't any of her business, and she should leave the whole situation alone, but try as she might she couldn't shake the feeling that she had failed Gracie in some way. She'd pushed so hard to convince her to join, and now only a few weeks in, just when she was really starting to show some progress, she'd been pulled away.

With no Gracie left to teach, and her hand starting to ache, Abs figured it was time to call it a night, so she grabbed her things. After all, sitting around behind her desk, sulking about the fact that Gracie was pulled out of classes with her, wasn't   going   to   change   things.

Seven

Abs tried to forget about Gracie over the next week. There was still a nagging part of the back of her head that felt guilty for just letting Hayley walk out of there with her daughter, but Abs knew there was nothing she could do about it. Besides, she was a little annoyed that Gracie had lied to her—she'd even asked her if Hayley knew about the classes, and she'd told her that she did, and there was no problem. With that assurance, how was Abs the one to blame for what had happened?

There was plenty going on to keep her occupied with Gracie's absence though. The gym was packed most evenings, and it was a mixture of those there for the sheer joy of fitness as well as those training to compete. Abs and the other trainers were swamped trying to keep the serious contenders on their toes and make sure they were on form, as well as the routine classes and members. At the end of most evenings, she was so busy and exhausted that she had neither the time nor the energy to worry about Gracie.

The pain in her hand was becoming a more regular occurrence. It still wasn't as bad as it had been when Abs had first recovered from the accident, but the little twinges of sharp, stinging pain that shot through her wrist and fingers made her wince every so often. It wouldn't have been too much of a problem, but every time it happened, Abs would catch Logan shooting her concerned looks out of the corner of her eye.

She knew that she should see a doctor about it. There was a pretty steady pain level that she'd grown accustomed to over the past few years, and every so often she'd have flare-ups that were just a little worse than normal. They'd go away, she'd forget about them, and then she'd go on with her life. But recently, it felt like she was experiencing flare-ups every other day.

The idea of going back to a doctor terrified her—not that she'd tell Logan that, of course. The mere thought of walking into another doctor's office, only to be told she'd need yet another operation, or maybe even lose more of the dexterity in her hand, was too much to bear. It brought back all the memories of her recovery from the accident, all the weeks she'd spent laying in bed with nothing to do but stare at the ceiling.

Instead, she tried to hide it. She threw herself into the training, concentrating on making sure that the women who came to the gym were pushing themselves as hard as they could. Some people had accused her of reliving her fighting career through the women she helped train, and at times like these, they were almost certainly right. But it kept Abs's mind off the pain in her hand, and it stopped her from thinking about Gracie, so she didn't care all that much.

It was a week before she showed up again. Abs was training one of their fresh young starters, Casey, with boxing mitts. They were working on her accuracy. Abs was making a mental note of every hit that was sloppy, and every punch that was just a little off-center. Her footwork was fine, she was plenty fast, but none of that would matter much given how poor her accuracy was.

She was so focused on the training that she didn't even register the door opening in her peripheral vision. It was only when Logan called her name that she paused the training, taking a moment to shake out her hands.

"Hey, Abs!" Logan called.

"Yeah?" Abs grunted. She pulled off the sparring mitts and tossed them to the floor, then rubbed her wrists.

"Isn't that the kid you invited here? I thought she wasn't supposed to be getting classes anymore?" Logan asked, nodding over to the corner of the room.

"What kid?" Abs asked, without looking up. Before Logan could respond, she realized exactly who the other woman was talking about. Gracie.

"Oh, shit." Abs groaned, looking up.

Please don't let that be Gracie. Please.

But of course, when Abs lifted her head and looked up, there Gracie was at the edge of the room. She was already dressed in her gym gear, clutching the handle of her backpack between her hands. When she saw Abs looking at her, she raised one hand in an uncertain, sheepish wave.

"Hi," she called, smiling gently.

Shit.

Abs was beyond screwed if Hayley found out about this. Fuck it, they'd *both* be screwed.

"Gracie." She sighed, ducking under the ropes of the boxing ring. "You know you shouldn't be here."

The smile slipped from Gracie's face and morphed into a scowl. As Abs got closer, Gracie rolled her eyes. "What, because my mom said I can't come?"

"Well...I mean, yeah."

"Are you scared of her?"

"Are you *not*?" Abs countered. When Gracie didn't look any more impressed, she decided to change tack. It didn't really matter *how* she got Gracie out of the gym, only that she did so. "Listen, I'd love for you to be able to stay and train here. I really would. But I'm not your mom, and I'm not going to go behind her back like this."

"But if she doesn't *know*—"

"Gracie," Abs said sharply. "I said no. It's an insult to your mom to lie to her like this. She's got her reasons for not wanting you here. Now, I might not agree with them, but I'm sure as hell gonna respect them. And you should too."

"But it's dumb!" Gracie cried out, all but stamping her feet. "You know it is too!"

By now, she'd made enough noise and fuss that other heads had turned. The image of a grown woman standing

50

around and arguing with a teenager wasn't exactly a good look for her, and Abs felt heat rising up the back of her neck.

"We're calling you a ride," she said, pulling her cell phone out of the back pocket of her leggings. Abs hit the Uber app and handed the phone to Gracie. "Put in your mum's address."

Gracie begrudgingly took the phone and started to type. Abs watched her but was distracted by a voice in the lobby. It was slightly muffled by the door, but Abs could still tell that whoever it was, they were seriously pissed off about something.

"She's here! Isn't she?"

The door from the lobby into the gym burst open, and Abs cringed at the sound of the wood smacking into the wall.

God, please don't let that be who I think it is.

Luck wasn't on her side though. Sure enough, Hayley was on the other side of it. If the rest of the gym hadn't been silent already, it certainly was now at the sight of an irate woman in the doorway.

Hayley scanned the room, and when she saw her daughter, Abs swore she saw a genuine fire in the other woman's eyes.

"Gracie," she hissed, marching over and closing the gap between them surprisingly quick. "What the hell do you think you're doing here? I told you I didn't want you coming here again!"

"Mom—" Gracie tried to protest, but Hayley cut across her sharply.

"I don't want to hear it. Go and wait for me out in the lobby."

Gracie turned her gaze on Abs, silently pleading with her to offer a helping hand. Abs felt the same guilt she had the first time Hayley had come in here. She wanted to help, she really did. She wanted to defend Gracie, she wanted to fight, to argue back against Hayley. But ultimately, she knew it wasn't her place to do so. As much as Abs hated to admit it, she knew she had no right to keep Gracie here with her. This was Hayley's home turf, and her decision was final.

The room was uncomfortably silent as Gracie gave in and walked away from them, sparing her mother a quick glare as she did so. Once she was out of earshot, Hayley turned those fiery eyes on Abs.

"*You*," she hissed, her voice dangerously low. She took a step towards Abs, and although Abs's instinct was to take a step backwards to compensate, she held her ground. "How *dare* you? I made it perfectly clear to you last time I was here that I wanted you to have nothing more to do with my daughter. Who do you think you are, letting her come back here, and encouraging her to sneak around me like this? I'm her *mother!*"

That got Abs's back up. Of course, Hayley had no idea that she had actually been trying to get rid of Gracie, but maybe if she'd just bothered to ask, rather than storming the place like a god-damn SWAT operative, she wouldn't have her panties in a twist. What was Abs supposed to do? Fit Gracie with a tracker so that she'd know when the kid was within fifty feet of the gym?

"Listen, Hayley—" she began, but before she could get out another word, or explain herself, pain exploded across her left cheek, and her head snapped to one side sharply. Abs gasped, a mixture of pain and surprise. As she reeled backwards, she heard hushed whispers from around the room.

Did she just slap me?

That was the only mildly coherent thought Abs could come up with.

For a moment, she saw red, but her boxer's instinct of discipline kicked in. Even though her body was coursing with adrenaline, she straightened up and looked Hayley in the eye.

Hayley looked horrified by what she'd done. There was a genuine look of revulsion on her face as she realized she'd lashed out. As Abs straightened up, Hayley took a small step backwards.

In her peripheral vision, Abs saw Logan approaching, already prepared to break things up if Hayley tried anything else. Abs held her hand out to the side as a silent command for her to stop. It was okay, she could tell just from looking at Hayley. The other woman had no intention of doing anything else.

"I think it's probably best that you leave, Hayley," Abs said finally, motioning towards the door.

All the self-righteous anger and maternal defensiveness that had carried Hayley into the gym had just dissipated with that one slap. She seemed to deflate in front of Abs's eyes, shrinking back into just a shell. She couldn't even meet her gaze as she took a couple of small steps back towards the door, and then she nodded.

"Yeah," she whispered. "I...yeah."

With that, Hayley turned on her heel and fled, pushing past a stunned client on her way out. The door slammed shut behind her, leaving the gym in a heavy, pointed silence that was just *suffocating*. There was only one thing on everyone's mind, and although everyone knew they were all thinking the same thing, not one of them dared say it out loud.

A woman had just walked into the gym, assaulted one of the trainers, and then left. All in the space of less than a couple of minutes.

"You good?" Logan asked hesitantly, looking Abs up and down. "That woman is—"

"She's not crazy," Abs said, cutting her off.

"What the hell was that about? She just slapped you." Sapphy, being Sapphy, had to state the obvious.

"Nothing—it's nothing. Nothing happened."

"She just *assaulted* you, Abs," Logan exclaimed in exasperation.

Abs pressed a hand to her cheek, where she could already feel the skin growing hot. It stung to touch it. She pulled her hand away quickly. For someone who claimed that she didn't believe in violence, Hayley sure seemed to pack quite the punch.

"I'm fine." Abs shrugged it off, surprising even herself with how nonchalant she felt about this whole thing. If it were anyone else, would she react like this? If any other person had stormed into the gym and slapped her, would she be casually chatting with her friend, or would she be filing a complaint?

She shook her head slowly, sighing. Around them, the rest of the gym was starting to return to normal, which was good. A few people were still shooting her uncertain glances out of the corner of their eyes, or even whispering among themselves, but most of them had returned to whatever it was they were doing.

Good.

"Just forget about it," Abs said quietly, heading for the lobby. Unsurprisingly, Sapphy ignored that and followed her out.

"Forget about it?" she echoed. "*Forget about it*? Why are you defending this woman?"

Abs sighed, leaning on the front desk. Out of the corner of her eye, she spotted her cell phone. Gracie must have dropped off for her before she was hauled out of the building. She picked the phone up and stuffed it into the back pocket of her leggings, before turning back to face Sapphy. Her best friend was still waiting expectantly for an answer.

The only problem was, Abs didn't have one for her. Not one that made sense, anyway. Hell, even she didn't really understand why she was defending this woman so ardently. She only knew that for some reason, despite how stubborn and boneheaded and downright *wrong* Hayley was, there was something about her that she liked. That wasn't exactly a defense that would stand up in Sapphy's eyes though.

"*Well?*" she prompted, folding her arms.

"What do you want me to tell you? She's stressed. She freaked out. She thinks she's doing what's right for her kid, and I don't think we should crucify her for that."

"I'm not saying we should crucify her. I'm saying that maybe we stop her from... oh, I don't know, *slapping the shit* out of my staff?"

Abs knew why Sapphy was angry. Hell, if the tables were turned, she would probably be just as angry, and it would be just as reasonable. In Sapphy's eyes, Abs was letting this stranger walk all over her and by extension, everyone else that worked there.

"She wasn't going after the rest of the staff," Abs reminded her quietly. "She only has a problem with me."

Sapphy opened her mouth to retort, but nothing came out. She was, possibly for the first time since they'd met, completely and totally lost for words.

"I don't want a big deal made of this." Abs raised her hand as Sapphy went to speak. "It'll be fine, just as long as Gracie doesn't sneak back in here again." Abs offered her friend a small smile, but it didn't really do much to comfort either of them. "But I, uh...I think I'm going to head home. Can you get Logan to finish up with Casey?"

"Hmm, I can't really say 'no' to that, can I?"

It was obvious Sapphy wasn't done with this conversation, not entirely. There was more she wanted to say, more she wanted to argue about. She wanted to know why Abs was so calm about all this, why she was defending Hayley despite the fact that the other woman had literally just assaulted her in her own workplace. But she'd known Abs for too long. She knew that standing in the lobby would do nothing and get her nowhere. Instead, she just let Abs go, and headed back into the main hall of the gym to sort out the remainder of Casey's session.

After she left, Abs unlocked her phone, bringing up the Uber app that Gracie hadn't closed before she'd left with her mom. It was still there, with the address to her mom's place still plugged in, just waiting for her to call for a ride.

Hayley didn't live far from Abs. In fact, she'd actually pass by their place on her way home. And for a moment, Abs considered what to do next. She wanted to try to talk to Hayley—preferably without getting hit again. But perhaps following her home before she'd even had the time to calm down wasn't the best call ever.

Abs tucked her phone away before heading out to the car. She could give Hayley some time to simmer down, maybe wait until the weekend, and then she would go and talk to her about the classes. This was a good opportunity for Gracie. It was obviously something she wanted to do, given that she'd come down there without Hayley's permission. Abs knew that it was good, but she just didn't know how to make Hayley understand that too. She had until the weekend to figure it out though. Hopefully that would be enough time.

With a sigh, Abs closed the Uber app and tossed her phone onto the passenger seat before heading home.

Eight

When Saturday rolled around, Abs decided to pay Gracie and Hayley a visit. Enough time had passed so she figured that they might be able to have a civil conversation, at the very least.

Abs drove to their street, and pulled up in front of the house she'd dropped Gracie off at before, staring at the doorway like she could see through it and somehow judge Hayley's mood. Now that Abs was in front of the house, she was suddenly nervous.

What was she supposed to say that hadn't already been said? Did she really think doggedly pursuing this was going to win Hayley over? Or would it just blow up in her face and end with her getting slapped again?

For a moment, Abs seriously thought about just leaving without going up to the door, but as her hand fell to the gear stick, she stopped herself. *No.* She'd come this far, she ought to see it through. She owed that to Gracie, at least.

Bracing herself for another argument, Abs stepped out of the car and headed up to the door of Hayley's place. She knocked twice and heard some shuffling around inside. Then, the door swung open to reveal Hayley on the other side.

The polite smile that was on Hayley's face vanished as soon as she realized who was on the other side of the door, replaced by a look of shock. Her mouth dropped open and her eyes widened in realization.

"Oh," she whispered. "It's you."

It wasn't exactly the warmest of welcomes, but nonetheless, Abs persevered. "Hey, Hayley."

"What—What are you doing here? How did you know where we live?"

"Relax…" Abs held her hands up. Jesus, the poor woman must have thought she was some kind of insane stalker. "I've dropped Hayley off here before, after class. And I just wanted to talk to you, if that's okay. Preferably, without you slapping me again."

Hayley's cheeks flushed pink, and she ducked her head, avoiding Abs's gaze. Clearing her throat, she took a step backwards, opening the door a little wider.

"Come in," she offered quietly. Abs stepped inside, shooting her a small smile. As she closed the door, Abs took a moment to look around.

It was a nice place, a little messy and unkempt, but hey, whose place wasn't?

"Sorry about the mess." Hayley must have seen her looking around, because she seemed even more embarrassed now. "I've been covering a lot of sick leave at work this week, so I've ended up doing some really crappy shifts."

"Yeah, Gracie said you worked in, uh…"

"Emergency dispatch, yeah." Hayley smiled weakly, but didn't say anything else about her job. To be fair to her, she didn't really *have* to say anything more; what else was there to be said? It was obvious what her job involved.

"Must be, uh—" Abs faltered. There wasn't really a word that seemed appropriate here. Interesting? Exciting? She spent all day listening to people at their most panicked and desperate; there wasn't much that could be said about that.

"Yeah," Hayley murmured, and the two fell into an uncomfortable silence. "Gracie isn't home, by the way."

"No?"

"She's at a friend's house."

"Oh, cool. Well, I mean, I came here to talk to you, anyway."

Maybe it was better that Gracie wasn't here. At least this way they could talk as two adults, without worrying about her interrupting or getting annoyed with them.

Immediately though, Hayley was on the defensive, like she knew exactly what the conversation was going to be about. Her mouth set into one thin line, and she folded her arms over her chest. "Oh. I get it, you're here to try to tell me why I should let Gracie come back to your classes."

"Well, I mean, yeah." Abs admitted. "What did you think I came here to do?"

"I *thought* you came here to apologize."

"Apologize?" Abs echoed. *Was this woman serious?* "Hey, I'm not the one who slapped another person for no reason. Which, by the way, was pretty rich coming from the woman who 'doesn't believe in violence'."

That subtle pink hue of Hayley's cheeks was bright red now, and she spluttered for a moment, struggling for a comeback. She couldn't think of one and fell silent for a few seconds.

"It's not your job," she said finally, with a shake of her head.

"Excuse me?" Abs was now seriously beginning to wonder whether her coming here was a good idea or even a rational one.

"It's not your job to...to 'parent' her. Okay? I know what's best for her, I know what she needs, and she *doesn't* need you to teach her how to be some reckless little thug that gets into fights with everyone she meets."

This woman was *impossible*. Abs was starting to regret defending her to Logan. Even if she was pretty, she was damned stubborn even when she was wrong.

"Well, I don't know if you're that good of a parent, given how long it took you to realize she was even *at* the gym."

That was a low blow. Fuck, that was an *awful* thing to say, and as soon as the words came out of her mouth Abs regretted them. Hayley's mouth dropped open, but she couldn't say anything. What could she possibly say after *that*? Abs wouldn't have been entirely surprised if she'd just decided to slap her.

"I didn't mean that," she said quietly, as Hayley took a step towards her. "I don't know why I said that. I'm sorry."

Hayley stopped right in front of her. The woman's breathing was shallow, her eyes blazed, and for a moment Abs thought she was about to get slapped again. But then, Hayley did something that took her completely by surprise.

She kissed her.

It took Abs a few seconds to register what was happening when she felt Hayley's lips pressed against hers. It was like her brain needed to take a moment to put all the pieces together, because what was happening just *didn't make any sense.*

No one was yelling.

They'd stopped fighting altogether.

There were hands on her cheeks.

Hayley's lips were against hers, and her tongue was gently coaxing her mouth open.

Hayley was kissing her.

Hayley. The same Hayley who had yelled at her in front of half the gym, and had slapped her, and had told her under no uncertain terms to stay away from her family—that same Hayley was kissing her right now?

What the fuck?

That was the rational part of Abs's brain *finally* catching up and kicking into gear, and when it did, Abs did the sensible thing and pushed Hayley backwards gently, easing her away with a hand on each shoulder. The two parted, and as they did, Abs realized that the woman in front of her was nothing like the morally upright, PTA worthy mother who she'd been arguing with only a few moments earlier.

Her pupils were blown wide, so much so that her irises were just thin slivers of blue. Her mouth hung open just a little, the apples of her cheeks were flushed pink, and her breathing was coming faster and heavier. Who the hell *was* this in front of her?

"Hayley…" Abs breathed out, but before she could say anything more, Hayley had her backed up against the wall of the hallway. Her lips were on Abs's again, and there was even more force behind the kiss now, even more passion. One of her hands cupped the back of Abs's head, her fingers weaving into the short locks of Abs's blonde hair, and the other slid down her body, coming to rest on the curve of her lower back.

There was still that little voice in the back of Abs's head, trying to tell her that this was decidedly a *bad* idea. That voice was trying to tell her to stop this, to cut this off before things went so far there was no coming back for either of them. It was her voice of reason, it was her conscious.

But then Abs heard Hayley moan gently into her mouth, and then her hand was under Abs's shirt. She was sandwiched between the hard plaster of the wall and the soft curves of Hayley's body. It was all just *too much*. She couldn't think anymore. She didn't *want* to think anymore. And when Hayley's cool hand slid up her stomach to graze over the fabric of her bra, that voice faded into nothing.

She didn't care that it was a bad idea.

She didn't care that this was probably wrecking her argument to let Gracie keep coming to the gym.

She didn't care about any of the consequences.

How could she, when she felt Hayley's hand move back down her body to rest on the zipper of her jeans?

*Fuck it,*was the final thought that went through her mind before she just gave in.

Hayley's fingers pressed against the cotton of her boxers, causing her to release a long moan. It had been almost six months since Abs had been with anyone, and her body was responding with hunger. Cupping Hayley's cheeks in her hands, she kissed her deeply. The softness of her full lips against her own; the sweet scent of coconut from her hair. Abs's head spun. This woman was intoxicating, and she had only started to drink her in.

"Where's your bedroom?" Her voice was low, and the tone amplified the need coursing through her body.

Hayley nodded to a door over to the right. Abs glanced over and then turned back to Hayley, staring straight into her soul. Letting her fingers trace the soft skin of her neck, she allowed her gaze to fall onto the beautiful curves of her breasts, stomach, and hips. Abs took in a deep breath, savoring the woman in front of her. Hayley was everything Abs craved. Soft, voluptuous curves that yielded to her touch; not like her hard taught muscles with no give.

There was something generous and inviting about Hayley's body that made Abs desperate to devour it, but before she could relish the thought further, she found herself being drawn back into a long, deep kiss. This was too much. She wanted Hayley, no; she needed her. She needed to feel her skin against Hayley's and the ever rising lust was demanding more with every fiber of her body.

Grabbing Hayley's ass, Abs lifted her, taking her weight as legs wrapped around her center. A shocked gasp, followed by an embarrassed giggle, erupted from Hayley's chest.

"Hold on tight." Abs chuckled, and she shuffled the pair of them towards the bedroom.

"I'll break your back, I'm—" Hayley's words withered away and her head dipped down into the hollow of Abs's neck.

"You are perfect," Abs whispered against Hayley's brown hair. "Absolutely perfect."

The door to the bedroom eased open, revealing a roughly made bed, and a slew of clothes hung over the back of a chair. With as much care as Abs's hunger would allow, she set Hayley down onto the edge of the bed. Leaning over, Abs placed a light kiss on her lips, pushing her down against the bed. This time, it was Abs's hands that explored Hayley's body, touching, stroking, caressing until the fervor between them had grown to fever pitch and the need to feel naked skin resulted in the ripping off of clothes.

Abs reveled in the sight of Hayley's naked body and the uncontrollable urgency to taste her burned so deeply she couldn't hold back another second. Dropping to her knees, she kissed the soft skin on the inside of Hayley's thighs and the shudder it elicited from her body made Abs smile. Lifting Hayley's legs over her shoulders, Abs let her lips work their way to the apex of Hayley's thighs, allowing her breath to tickle against her short, trimmed hair. Another shudder and moan escaped from Hayley's body. But it was nothing in comparison to the groan she let out in response to Abs's tongue as it slid through her hot, velvet folds.

To Abs, there was no better taste in the world than the subtle tang which was coating her tongue. Working her way up the slick, smooth warmth from her entrance to Hayley's swollen, throbbing clit, Abs made every second count. Her tongue expertly teased its way in swirls, moving from flat, broad strokes to tight, hard flicks. Hayley writhed in pleasure beneath her, her hips bucking and twisting with her every touch.

Grasping and looping her arms around her thighs to hold them tightly in place, Abs sunk deeper into Hayley's core. First, she took her hard nub, sucking it gently into her mouth, teasing Hayley to the point of excruciating pleasure. Then, using her shoulders to raise Hayley's hips a little higher, her tongue dove straight in, fucking her hard.

In what felt like no time, Hayley was squirming, screaming in rapture before her body tensed and shuddered as she gave into the crashing orgasm.

The tension gave way, replaced by a heavily satiated relaxation as Hayley sank into the white cotton comforter. Abs unhooked Hayley's legs from her shoulders and crawled up the bed to lie next to her. Running her fingers over her breasts, she watched Hayley's chest rise and fall as she tried to recover her breath. Tiny, spontaneous shudders exploded through her body, causing Abs to smile as she kissed her shoulder affectionately.

"I, oh, I—" Hayley's attempts at words crumbled as yet another series of tremors shook her foundation.

"Sh! Take your time." There was a soothing tone to the words which Abs spoke, and placing an arm over Hayley's naked body, she pulled her tight against her own warm skin.

After several moments, Hayley turned to face her, placing her hand on her cheek. After placing a light kiss on Abs's lips, she pulled back, coyly averting her eyes.

"Thank you," she whispered.

And then an odd – almost eerie – silence overcame them.

Nine

Hayley was the first to break the heavy silence that settled over them. What had erupted in a fierce passion that consumed them both, had now ended with an odd, awkward calm. While Abs was happy to allow the silence to settle, Hayley was obviously far less comfortable and she was the first to get out of bed, quickly searching for her clothes.

"Gracie will be home soon," she said quietly, pulling her dressing gown on. She tugged the fabric around herself in an attempt to cover up as much of her body as possible, but it wasn't much use. The dressing gown fell open a little at the front, exposing part of her chest, and showed off the marks that Abs had left against her skin.

That was Abs's cue to get dressed and get out of the house. It wasn't exactly a subtle one, and it was obvious that Hayley didn't want her to hang around for much longer. Hell, she didn't even want to look at her anymore. It was like she was a completely different person now. The woman who had pushed her up against the wall downstairs, the woman who had actually *initiated* sex, was long gone. All of that passion, that want, that *need*, all of that had just vanished. In fact, if Abs hadn't been *very present* for the past couple of hours, she probably wouldn't have believed the two of them had had sex.

Hayley hadn't gone back to the way she was acting around Abs before though. She didn't seem so aggressively stand-offish. If Abs didn't know any better, she'd say that Hayley actually seemed...embarrassed about the whole thing. She wasn't even able to meet Abs's gaze anymore and was focusing her gaze on the bedsheets.

It didn't matter that Hayley was hardly speaking though; it was obvious she regretted what had happened. Abs had been in this position with women before, and while everyone had different reactions to spur-of-the-moment sexual encounters, it was the first time anyone had reacted like *this*. It was the first time anyone had really looked like they'd regretted sleeping with Abs immediately after the fact.

Abs wasn't stupid. She knew when she wasn't wanted, and she also knew that overstaying her welcome with Hayley was only going to make things worse between them. So instead of arguing back, or suggesting that they perhaps talk about what had just happened, she got out of bed and started looking for her clothes. They were strewn all over the place, and she was pretty sure her t-shirt was still downstairs on the floor of the hall.

As she got dressed, Hayley cleared her throat. "This uh...this shouldn't happen again."

Abs couldn't agree more. This was a decidedly *bad* idea. The kind of bad idea that you saw in a movie right before you started screaming at the characters about how *stupid* they were being.

"Yeah."

"Gracie—it—would be bad. For her," Hayley said, frowning.

"Yeah, it would be." Abs zipped her jeans up and stuffed her hands deep into her pockets.

"So, we shouldn't—"

"No, we shouldn't."

Hayley turned to look at her. "So we both agree that this—"

"Was a bad idea," Abs finished for her. "Yeah."

"Okay." Hayley nodded slowly. "Okay."

Abs sighed heavily. This wasn't exactly how she'd expected her afternoon to turn out when she'd decided to come and see Hayley, and she was no closer to convincing her to let Gracie come back to the gym.

"Listen. Hayley—"

"Hmm?" She looked up, twisting the sash of her dressing gown around her hand over and over.

66

"Can you at least...think about letting Gracie come back to classes? I know I'm probably pushing my luck here, but I just...I know how much she enjoyed it, and I'd hate to have it taken away from her just 'cause it's not something you understand. I mean, when you were a teenager, did you ever have to give something up because your parents didn't approve?"

Hayley looked at her for a few moments with a strange expression on her face. She looked...softer, all of a sudden. Perhaps that was finally the thing that would get through to her, after all of Abs's attempts.

"You can come to one of the classes I run," Abs offered. "And you can see for yourself that there's nothing bad going on. After that, if you still aren't convinced, then I'll drop it. But I just...I don't want you to give up on this too easily."

"Fine," Hayley said, after another long pause. "I'll take Gracie to the session next week and...I'll watch. But if I don't like what I see—"

"Then you can feel free to hit me again." Abs stuck out her hand. It felt oddly formal to shake Hayley's hand given what they'd just done, but then again, this wasn't a particularly *normal* situation.

Hayley didn't exactly look amused by the joke, but she shook Abs's hand, regardless.

"We'll see you next week," she said quietly.

"Looking forward to it." Abs gave her a slight grin and nod   before   letting   herself   out.

67

Ten

Even though Hayley had agreed to come to the gym with Gracie, Abs still wasn't completely certain that she would follow through. She half expected them not to show up. After all, given what had happened on Saturday, it was just one more reason for Hayley to avoid her.

But then, to her surprise, they showed up on Wednesday afternoon.

Gracie all but ran into the gym, with Hayley trailing behind a little more hesitantly. She was looking around at the other trainers and clients, a little uncertain, hugging her arms around herself like a shield. Everyone else was too focused on doing their own thing to notice her walk in, let alone recognize her as the woman who had made such a scene the week before. But she still looked nervous.

As they approached Abs, she was still glancing around like she was worried someone was going to toss her out, and to be fair, her fears weren't entirely unfounded. More than once that week, Logan had threatened to ban her from stepping foot in the gym again. Abs had talked her down every time, thankfully.

"Look at you." Abs grinned at Gracie. "You're already dressed for class."

Gracie wasn't wearing her school gym uniform today—she was dressed in a big t-shirt and gym leggings, and a shiny new water bottle was swinging from her left hand, instead of the plastic water bottle from the vending machine that she just reused. From the looks of it, she'd strong armed her mom into getting her kitted out for classes.

When Hayley walked over to her, her greeting was less warm. She nodded to Abs briefly, meeting her gaze for a second before looking away again. Her gaze wandered over the inside of the gym, avoiding having to look Abs in the eye.

"Glad you decided to come," Abs said to her, almost immediately regretting her choice of words. A muscle jumped in Hayley's jaw, and her cheeks flushed red. To anyone else, that would have been a perfectly innocent statement, but to them? Not a chance.

Abs cleared her throat, turning back to Gracie. "Right, let's get started."

She'd done classes in front of parents before. It wasn't uncommon for an especially overprotective parent to hang around at the edge of the gym, watching on while *trying* to give their kid some space. Their presence could be limiting for their kid, but it was something Abs had grown accustomed to over the years that she'd been a trainer. But this time was going to be different, and Abs wasn't naïve enough to forget that.

She decided to start Gracie off with a warm up. It had been a while since they'd had a proper session together, so she wanted to ease her back into things. Gracie was given a jump rope and a set of instructions to keep her on her toes, and as she got started, Abs began walking around her, correcting her on her form. She needed to keep her head up and focus on something in the distance, like the clock above the entrance. Her back had to be straight, but not rigid.

Then, once Gracie started to get back into the swing of things, Abs had to give her less and less instruction. And as soon as that happened, she found herself looking over at Hayley, sneaking glances whenever she could. Abs knew that she shouldn't; Gracie was supposed to be the focus of the day, not Hayley, but try as she might her gaze seemed to wander back to Hayley.

Hayley wasn't looking at her though. Her gaze was always trained directly on Gracie, almost like she was deliberately trying not to look at Abs again. Was she thinking about what had happened between them?

Abs sure was, especially now, after that unfortunately phrasing.

Every time she looked over at Hayley, she'd feel the ghost of her touch against her skin, she'd see her arching her back, letting her head drop to the pillows, and she'd hear her breathless, desperate moans.

Focus, Abs. She scolded herself mentally. She hadn't invited Hayley here to indulge in the memory of the last time they'd met. They weren't there for that; they were there for *Gracie.* And besides, the deal had been that what had happened between the two of them was going to stay a secret. It was a onetime event, a mistake they'd never talk about again.

It was hard to focus on the class and not let her mind wander though. So instead of just standing around, Abs tried to keep herself busy. She figured maybe if she kept talking about Gracie's stance, her posture, her footwork – all decidedly safe topics – she wouldn't keep zoning out back to Hayley's bed.

"There are a lot of moving parts when it comes to boxing," she explained to Hayley, glancing over at her. "Probably the most common misconception about it is that it's all about how hard and fast you can hit the other person."

Hayley shifted on the spot, looking a little uncomfortable. Abs knew that had been exactly what she'd first thought of boxing, and Hayley had just about said as much. She met Abs's gaze for a second, but then looked away again just as quickly. That suited Abs just fine.

"There are a lot of different things going through your head when you're in the ring. There are so many things you have to consider if you want to win. You've got to think about what you're doing, whether your stance is right, because if it's not, then you're going to get knocked down pretty quick. You've got to think about what your opponent is doing in front of you, and what your opponent is *going to be doing.* And all that time, you've got to keep on your toes. You've got to keep moving, because it makes you a harder target. But then, you can't just start dancing around in a pattern like you're ballroom dancing, because your opponent will pick up on that, and they'd be able to time their punches. All of that's going through your head from the moment you step into the ring."

"Right." Hayley nodded alone, still looking at Gracie.

"That's why jump ropes are such a good call for warm-ups. They force you to move at a certain speed, to keep a rhythm, and to engage every muscle in one way or another. You have to have good focus, or else you'll trip and fall on your ass. Plus…it's good cardio," she finished lamely.

"Uh huh." Hayley nodded again.

Abs wasn't even sure whether she was really paying her any attention anymore, but it didn't matter that much to her. She was more concerned with keeping herself occupied.

"That's why they call it the 'sweet science'," she explained. "Because you've got to juggle all those different variables. Your mind is just as important as your body; maybe even more important, in some cases."

"The 'sweet science'…" Hayley repeated quietly.

She paused before looking over at Abs, and for the first time, she smiled. It was small, fleeting, and disappeared so quickly that Abs might have missed it if she hadn't been paying attention, but it was definitely there.

"I like that."

Was she finally getting through to her? Abs wasn't exactly ready to call it a victory just yet, but that little smile was a good sign. Maybe she was starting to warm up to the idea of letting Gracie take classes here.

The next exercise was the one Abs was a little more uncertain about. Target practice. She fetched a set of gloves and some target pads from the equipment cupboard, before heading back to Gracie.

"What's this?" Hayley asked, peering over at them curiously.

"When you box, you need precision," Abs explained, putting the target pads on. "Your punches aren't going to be worth all that much if you miss every shot you take."

"Abs says I'm a natural at this," Gracie called over at her mother.

It probably wasn't *too* helpful to Abs's case that Gracie excelled at the more physical side of things, but hey, everyone had a particular talent *somewhere*.

Gracie dropped into a fighter's stance before they began, and Abs was surprised to see just how well she was doing, despite how long since she had last practiced. Just like the jump rope, she was a little rusty to begin with, but soon warmed up and got back into the swing of things.

They went through some other exercises after that. Abs stuck her on the speed bag for a bit, and then went through a little more cardio and some core exercises, before deciding to call it a day. Gracie had done well for her first session back, and even though they'd been at it for over an hour, she wasn't showing any signs of slowing down. Despite her eagerness, Abs knew it was probably best to cut things off before Hayley got bored just standing there on the sidelines. She didn't want to put her off coming back.

Gracie went to shower, and when she did, Abs decided to take the chance to talk to Hayley in private. It was the first time they'd spoken to each other since Saturday, but surprisingly, despite how uncomfortable Hayley had been at the start, she seemed to have relaxed now.

"So, what do you think?" Abs asked. "Is this the violent, dangerous game that you thought it would be?"

Hayley's cheeks flushed pink again at that comment, and she laughed nervously, then shook her head. At least she had the good grace to look embarrassed. "No. No, I don't."

Abs offered her a kind smile. "You know, I don't really blame you for the way you felt about all this at the start."

"You don't?"

"No. It's...it's kind of how my mom felt when I began boxing."

"She didn't want you doing it either?" Hayley asked. She looked relieved to know that she wasn't the only parent who'd had reservations about the sport.

"Sure. I mean, she didn't slap my gym teacher..." Abs trailed off with a teasing smile. "But she didn't like the idea, not for a long time. But after a while, she came around. I think she realized that it was good for me to have this outlet, something to channel all my frustration into. I think she figured it was better for me to spend all my nights at a gym hitting a bag than getting involved with the neighborhood kids."

"How'd you convince her in the end?"

"I didn't." Abs admitted with a smile. "My gym teacher did. She told my mom that boxing isn't about fighting; it's about discipline. It gets this bad rep because everyone looks at hotshot professionals who are assholes to each other on TV, but it's so much more than that. I don't want to teach Gracie how to beat up other kids on the street, or start fights with everyone who pisses her off. I want her to be able to *respect* this, to realize that there's a difference between competing and scrapping with other people just because you're frustrated."

Hayley looked over at the door her daughter had just gone through, shifting around. It was obvious she still wasn't one hundred percent sold on the idea of putting Gracie in the ring, but it sure looked like she was coming around.

"Will it help her?" Hayley's brow furrowed with concern.

"I'm not saying she's going to become this perfect model child," Abs said gently. "She...hasn't had the easiest time, and I get that."

"She told me you'd met Ed." Hayley sighed.

"Yeah, and y'know...for the record, the guy is an asshole." Abs shot her another small smile, which she returned. "And Gracie is probably going to carry some shit

73

around for a while because of that. I'm not saying this is going to fix everything. A few sessions here don't come with a guarantee of A grades at school and perfect manners, but this *might* give her something to focus on. She's a teenager, she doesn't know how to cope with all the shit she's probably feeling. So maybe this will give her somewhere to direct all of that."

There was a silence following Abs's words, and it dawned on her she might have overstepped the mark. Had she gone way too far and stuck her nose into Hayley's family life where she wasn't wanted? Abs braced herself to get yelled at again. But to her surprise, Hayley didn't yell. She didn't even look annoyed. Instead, she looked grateful.

"If you think this might help her, then…then let's give it a shot," she said slowly, still looking a little hesitant.

Relief flooded through Abs's system, and she let out a nervous laugh. "You're serious? You'll let her come to train?"

"Yeah." Hayley nodded. "I'll let her come. But if she comes home injured, or it affects her behavior, I'm pulling her out."

"That's fair." Abs smiled. "You want to go tell her the good news? We can get her properly signed up."

Any last hints of awkwardness between the two of them disappeared as they headed out into the lobby to sign Gracie up for classes. Hayley filled out one of the emergency contact forms, and as she did, Abs had a thought. It was a stupid thought, given the fact that she was already treading on wafer thin ice around Hayley already, but she decided to chance it. What did she have to lose?

"I know this might be pushing my luck…" Abs began slowly. Hayley glanced up from the form. "But…have you thought about maybe doing something like this? For yourself?"

"Boxing?"

"I mean, you do throw a mean right hook," Abs teased.

"I said I was sorry about that." Hayley blushed.

"I'm sorry. I'll stop making jokes about that," Abs promised. "But seriously, have you thought about it? It's good for Gracie, and from what Gracie has told me about your job...maybe you might find it cathartic?"

She must have woken up with a golden tongue that morning, or maybe the quarter she'd picked up outside her place had really been lucky, because Hayley didn't just dismiss her straight away. Instead, she actually thought about it for a few moments.

"I..." She tilted her head to one side. "Maybe I will. I have Friday afternoon off, so...I might stop by, but I'm a bit out of shape."

"You will?" Abs asked, surprised. "We'd work at your level and build your fitness up, so don't worry about that."

"I *might*." She finished filling out the form, just as Gracie came back into the lobby. "Hey sweetheart, are you ready to go home?"

Gracie looked between the two of them expectantly. "So do I get to keep coming here? Do I get to train?"

Hayley smiled at her, putting an arm around her shoulder. "Oh, we'll see. We've got the whole ride home to talk about that. *And* your math homework..."

"That's not a no," Gracie pointed out.

"It's not, is it?" Hayley chuckled.

As they headed out of the front doors, they waved goodbye to Abs, who was still standing behind the desk. Abs watched as Hayley's gaze lingered on her for a few seconds before she stepped out of the door, as if there was something more she wanted to say, but didn't. And then she was gone, with Gracie in tow.

Eleven

Hayley started classes the next week. She seemed a little nervous around Abs at first, probably as a result of *the event that should never be named*, but once Abs got her started on some exercises, she relaxed into the swing of things. During their very first session together, when Abs asked her if there was anything in particular she wanted to work on, Hayley nervously pointed to her stomach, and patted her thighs.

"They're kind of..." She pulled a face. "Ugh, y'know?"

Abs could honestly say that she *didn't* know. She'd seen everything there was to see of Hayley, and there was *nothing* wrong with the way she looked. "You want to what? Tighten up your thighs and core?"

"I want a flatter stomach, like you..." Hayley gestured to Abs's perfectly flat stomach. "I like the...lines you have down the sides."

Abs tugged her t-shirt up a little. "My obliques?"

"Those." Hayley pointed to the obvious obliques showing on Abs's stomach. "I want those."

Abs assured her that there was nothing wrong with the way that she looked, but agreed that obliques exercises were something that they could factor into workouts. Honestly, she was more than a little envious of Hayley's body, but she knew if she said that Hayley would think she was lying. Abs wished she could have the hourglass curves that Hayley's fuller figure boasted however, she looked sort of like a plank. Sure, she had killer abs, but boobs? Not a chance. A waistline? Hardly.

We always want what we don't have, Abs mused.

The first few classes weren't very productive. Hayley was still getting used to the intensity of the workouts, and it was obvious that she wasn't exactly having the time of her life while she was sweating and panting. To her credit though, she stuck with it and carried on, regardless. As the weeks went by, Abs started to notice an improvement.

It probably wasn't something that Hayley herself had noticed, but when she walked into the gym, Abs would pick up on her posture. Her back was straight when she walked now, she seemed like she was carrying herself with a little more confidence. She was able to run for longer, and it wasn't long before she could hold a plank for a whole ninety seconds without begging to stop.

They had both agreed that *the event that should never be named* would never be repeated, and Abs was fully prepared to respect that. But that didn't mean it wasn't on her mind.

Most of the time, it was fine. *Most* of the time, they weren't actually in contact with each other. Hayley would work out, and Abs would give her pointers and encouragement. But *some* of the time, she needed to correct Hayley's posture, and that would involve the two of them getting a little closer.

Abs told herself that when she stood right behind Hayley and wrapped her arms around her, it was just so she could do her job. She assured herself that when she offered to tie Hayley's hair back from her face and spent a little longer than necessary combing her hands through her hair, she was just being thorough. But really, she just wanted an excuse to be closer to her.

She wasn't sure what it was about Hayley that kept pulling her in, but every time she took a class with her, Abs would find herself looking for any excuse to be close to her. When she'd straighten Hayley up and correct her posture, her hands would linger on the other woman's skin for just a little longer than necessary. She'd lean in closer than she had to so she could speak in her ear, so close that it was *almost* inappropriate, without ever quite crossing the line.

If Abs didn't know any better, she would have said that Hayley was doing the same thing. Sometimes she'd ask for help on exercise, where she already had perfect form, as if she was just asking Abs to come closer and watch her. If Abs walked off to talk to one of the other trainers and happened to glance back over, she'd often see Hayley looking at her from across the gym. She'd look away as soon as she realized she'd been spotted, but it was obvious she had been looking.

And yet, they hardly spoke to each other. Besides a few pleasantries here and there during classes, Hayley barely spoke a word to her. Which was why, when Gracie's birthday rolled around, Abs was so surprised to get an invitation.

"Gracie would really like it if you showed up. It's just a small party, a few friends are coming over and eating, and then they're going bowling," Hayley told her after one of their classes together. "But I think she'd appreciate seeing you there."

Abs had to admit, she was glad to hear Gracie actually had some friends her own age. It probably wasn't great how she was spending most of her time around people who were twice her age, so Abs figured it would be nice to see her being a kid.

Of course, she was turning fourteen, so in her eyes she wasn't a *kid*, she was just an adult who still got treated like one. In honor of that (and because she honestly had no idea what fourteen-year-old girls actually liked), Abs decided that her gift to Gracie would be free membership to the gym for a year which gave her free run of all the equipment any time she wanted.

It wasn't as cool as the makeup Gracie's friends bought her, or the clothes Hayley had wrapped up so neatly, but it still earned her a high five and a hug when Gracie opened her birthday card and saw her gym membership inside. Seeing her grin at the little plastic card was more than enough for Abs.

The party didn't last long. As Hayley had pointed out to Abs earlier, the main event was that Gracie was going bowling with her friends (apparently kids still liked bowling), and then they were going to have pizza at the diner nearby.

They were mainly there so that Gracie could rip open all her presents, toss wrapping paper all over the front room, and then blow out her candles. One slice of ice cream cake later, the kids were all rushing out to go bowling.

She was the last guest to leave, and although Hayley had told her that it was fine to go, she paused in the doorway of the front room. There was wrapping paper on every conceivable surface, and there were paper plates scattered around the room, with remnants of food and cake.

"Are you sure you don't want a hand?" Abs asked. "This is a lot to clear up."

"It's part of the job." Hayley already had a bag in her hand and was beginning to pick her way through the mountain of rubbish. She was probably right, she probably *could* handle it just fine, but Abs still felt guilty about leaving her to clear it up on her own.

"The trash bags are in the kitchen, right?" Abs asked, tossing her jacket back on the coat rack by the door. She made her way into the kitchen without waiting for an answer, even while Hayley was calling that she didn't have to.

"I can do it, you're a *guest,*" she chided as Abs returned to the front room.

"I'm also a grown up. C'mon, I'm not totally useless when it comes to clearing up."

Hayley took one look at the paper strewn around the room and gave in. "Start over there."

"Yes Ma'am."

Abs followed her directions and went to the couch, which she could hardly see under strips of pink tissue paper. As she worked, she could have sworn she felt Hayley's eyes on her, but when she glanced back at the other woman, she was busy clearing up.

The two of them worked in silence to clear the front room. Abs tried to make conversation a few times, but she couldn't keep Hayley talking for more than a couple of minutes before they would just fall into another uncomfortable silence.

"Gracie seems to be doing well now," Abs said eventually. There had to be something she could do to shatter the awkward tension in the room and talking about her daughter seemed like a good way to break the ice.

"Hmm?" Hayley glanced over at her.

"It looks like she's happier now. I remember when I met her for the first time, it was like…she was kind of…" Abs fumbled for the right word. "I don't know…cold? Kind of stand-offish. But it looks like she's happy now, though. She's hanging out with friends…she's got hobbies…"

"She is," Hayley said, not quite meeting Abs's gaze. She had her back to Abs, and her shoulders were hunched up towards her ears. Even from behind, she looked stressed.

It was the first time they'd really been alone together since the day Abs had come to the house to convince Hayley that she was wrong about the classes. Sure, they'd seen each other since then; they'd had private classes at the gym; they'd had a few conversations, but they hadn't ever been alone, not really. Now there was no one in Abs's peripheral vision, they couldn't hear idle chatter or the dull smack of a fist hitting a vinyl punching bag. There were no distractions, nothing. Just them, and the tension that was almost overwhelming.

The atmosphere was almost thick with that tension; it was almost like the uncomfortable silence that had fallen over them after they'd had sex. There was that same heaviness in the air between them, the same sickly uncertainty.

Was this just how things were going to be between them now? Whenever they were left alone, they would have to suffer through this suffocating silence.

No, Abs decided. *Fuck that.* It wasn't fair to either of them to tiptoe around what had happened. They were both adults, and they needed to act like it.

"Alright," she said finally, dumping the bag full of wrapping paper on the floor before folding her arms. "It's time to cut the shit, Hayley."

That caught her attention, if nothing else had done. Hayley's head snapped up, probably more on instinct than anything else, and she looked over sharply.

"Excuse me?"

Abs recognized that icy tone. She'd heard it enough times when the two of them had argued before to know that she was stepping into dangerous territory here, but she didn't care. She wasn't in the mood to keep dancing around this issue, and if Hayley got her way, it didn't look like they would ever sort this out.

"You heard me," Abs said, folding her arms. "This isn't going to work out if you just clam up on me every time we're alone together."

Hayley's mouth dropped open as she made an indignant noise. "I'm not—"

"Yes, you *are*," Abs stressed. "I mean, you're barely even looking at me right now!"

"So?"

"Oh, Jesus Christ..." Abs raked a hand through her blonde hair, the longer length on top flopped to one side as she let out a frustrated huff of air. "I get it, okay? You don't want what happened between us to happen again. You think it was a mistake. I *get* that, so you don't need to keep giving me the silent treatment here. I mean, what was the point of you coming to the gym, inviting me here, if the second we're alone you just shut down like this? I mean, I thought we were *good*."

Abs had thought that the atmosphere couldn't get any worse in the front room, but in the wake of her exasperated rant, the heavy silence was *unbearable*. After a few seconds, Abs felt herself deflate as frustration seeped out of her, and she began to feel a little guilty instead. Hayley didn't need her getting pissed off and yelling on top of everything else that was going on.

She opened her mouth to apologize for her outburst, but before she could, Hayley spoke up.

"It wasn't a mistake."

For a second, Abs thought she had misheard her. She figured that maybe her brain was just filling in the gaps, or perhaps it was just wishful thinking, because that made so much more sense to her. Did Hayley really believe that it wasn't a mistake? But what about the immediate awkwardness afterwards? The way she practically kicked her out of her bed? Hayley had all but ignored her...but it wasn't a mistake?

Her mind was playing tricks on her. Or her ears were; one or the other.

"Huh?"

She looked up, surprised to see that Hayley was looking at her from across the front room, meeting her gaze properly. There was no hesitation in her eyes now, none of the nervousness that Abs had seen so many times.

For a few seconds, she said nothing. Her eyes narrowed a little, as if she was considering her next move, and her tongue poked out to wet her lower lip. Then, without another word, she crossed the room and did something that surprised Abs even more.

She kissed her. It was quick and chaste, nothing more than a peck on the lips. But it was a kiss, there was no mistaking that.

"It wasn't a mistake," she repeated quietly, pulling back just enough so she could speak.

"But then why—" Abs began, but she didn't get the chance to finish her sentence. Hayley cut her off with another kiss, a proper one this time. She caught Abs's lips with her own, and just like the first time they had kissed, one hand cupped the back of Abs's head.

"Don't talk," she whispered in Abs's ear. "Don't say anything. I don't want to talk right now, I just want..." She drew in a shaky breath, and Abs felt her other hand tremble as it came to rest on her cheek. "The way you made me feel...I want to feel like that again. I want you to touch me the way you did before."

She pulled back to look Abs in the eye. Her cheeks were flushed, her breath was heavy, and her eyes were dark, all just like the last time Abs had found herself in Hayley's home. As they looked at each other, Hayley could only manage to say one other word.

"Please."

And with a request like that, how could Abs possibly refuse?

The tension that had been growing every time they had seen each other, spent time in each other's company, had coupled with the stolen glances to a point where they could no longer hold it back. Their clothes were strewn over the room as the urge to consume each other took hold, and by the time they reached the sofa they were both naked and shivering with desire.

Standing behind Hayley, Abs placed her hands on Hayley's hips. She drew her body closer so Hayley's buttocks were tight against her own thighs. There was barely a whisper between them. Moving Hayley's hair to the side, Abs placed light kisses on the nape of her neck. Small murmurs of pleasure from Hayley lay gently on the hushed air. Abs slipped her hands around Hayley's waist, her fingertips traversing down towards the top of her thighs.

As her light touch went through short hair, Hayley moaned in anticipation. The sound intensified and added to her own excitement as she delved lower, parting Hayley's soft, full lips. Abs inhaled her scent. The delicate vanilla filled with the heady musk of her body made Abs's head spin. *God, I want this woman.* From the wet readiness that coated Abs's fingers, it was evident that the desire was mutual.

Wasting no more time, Abs bent Hayley's body forward over the arm of the sofa. Hayley's ass was high and proud in the air causing Abs found her breath hitch with excitement. With one deep inhalation of anticipation Abs allowed her fingers to run the full length of Hayley's center. She was wet and ready, but Abs didn't want to rush the moment.

The discipline she had developed in training seeped into every area of her life, but in no other area was the effect so powerful. Using her knees, she pushed Hayley's legs wider. Her fingers continued to tease and explore every inch of Hayley's folds until she was twitching and squirming, desperate to be taken.

Then, without any warning, Abs placed two fingers over Hayley's entrance and used the weight of her body behind her hand to push hard and deep inside. The gasp and long groan that followed erupted in unison from their bodies, which cracked through the air with as much speed as the jolt of electricity that spread throughout their bodies. The rhythm moved from firm and slow to hard and unrelenting. With each thrust and moan, Hayley's body yielded with want. The unforgiving, relentless rhythm heightened the need further until Abs had four fingers pounded in and out, out and in. With her fingertips curled, pressing hard against Hayley's G-spot, their bodies moved together as one hot, wet, sweating mass of pleasure.

A high-pitched cry filled the room as the flood of orgasm swept through Hayley's body, causing it to clench tightly around Abs's fingers. And then as fast as it came, the orgasm dissipated, leaving in its trail fast, intense, shuddering reminders.

Abs raised Hayley from the sofa and embraced her. Light kisses replaced the spaces where words might have been and their bodies melded together with a building fervor once again. But this time, it was Hayley who was driving them forward. Pushing Abs back towards the sofa until her calves were pinned against the cushions, Hayley tried to push Abs to sit, but try as she might, Hayley remained standing.

"You're not making this easy for me, are you?" Hayley laughed, her cheeks flushing.

"It's the joy of having a strong core. I'm never a push over," Abs said with a lopsided grin. "Ask me nicely and—"

"Please?" Hayley's pitch raised at the end, her expression playfully pleading. It worked as Abs smiled and sat down on the edge of the sofa.

Hayley lowered herself down and kneeled between Abs's firm thighs. Abs mused at the intense look of concentration on her face as hands pushed her legs wider apart. Hayley was fixated on her core, which was now gleaming with desire. She watched Hayley's tongue slightly protrude and run along her bottom lips. A twitch of yearning pulsed at her very core and her breath hitched as it left her body in one long, slow beat.

Whereas Abs had opted to take her time and tease out every moment, Hayley didn't. Abs gasped as Hayley pushed her legs wide and with a long, broad, slow pass of her tongue, worked her way from the bottom of her center to her twitching nub. A moan followed as she felt her already swollen clit being taken into Hayley's mouth and sucked gently, then harder.

As fingers entered her and tongue teased, Abs began to feel herself quickly unravel. It wasn't just that it had been so long, it was this woman, her curves, her softness. In one long, low, guttural moan, Abs grasped handfuls of Hayley's hair, as she came in a burst of violent spasm and tremors.

"Fuck—fuck—fuck!"

Her eyes closed, with her head thrown back and chest tight, unable to inhale. Abs did the only thing she could and surrendered to the sensation. It was several minutes later that her body returned to breathing normally and when she lowered her head, she saw Hayley's gleaming face smiling up at her. With a laugh, she pulled her up and into her arms and they lay along the sofa, holding each other tightly.

Things between them were very different from last time. There wasn't that strange awkwardness, and Hayley certainly didn't push Abs towards the door. Instead, they just lay there together, wrapped in each other's arms. Neither of them really wanted to address what had happened, but they didn't really feel like they had to either.

When Abs eventually left a few hours later, Hayley kissed her goodbye and slipped a scrap of paper into her hand. Her phone number was written on it.

Twelve

Three days later, Abs got a text from Hayley asking if she was busy. She wasn't, and when she went over to Hayley's place, the two ended up in bed together. The same thing happened that weekend, when Gracie was out with friends at the movies. And then again, and again, and again. But Hayley never brought up the possibility of them having anything more together. As far as she was concerned, it was just about sex. Sex that no one else was going to know about, *especially* not her daughter.

Abs was perfectly happy with whatever arrangement they'd managed to strike up. Hayley was beautiful (despite the comments she made about herself at the gym), and a casual, stress free fuck buddy relationship that didn't really have any negatives to it in Abs's mind. Things carried on like that between the two of them for another few weeks until one night she got a text from Hayley while she was at the bar with Logan and some of the other trainers.

While she'd been bringing the round of drinks back from the table, Abs had felt her cell phone buzzing in her pocket. She'd missed a call, and possibly a text too from the feel of things. Once she'd handed everyone's drinks out and brought the tray back to the bartender, she pulled her phone out to check who wanted her attention so badly.

The text was from Hayley, the missed call was too. Something was up; since the two of them had slept together, Hayley was putting distance between them. She opened the message to see what Hayley wanted and was surprised by the message.

You busy?

That was all it said. Nothing about 'Hey, come over', or 'Hey, Gracie isn't home right now…' There were none of the normal innuendos or jokes that usually came with one of her invitations.

"You alright?"

Abs barely even heard Logan's voice as she looked at the message, a little confused. She texted back a quick *What's up?* only to see that the message was read immediately. Hayley must have had their messages open, and in a few seconds, she saw the tell-tale three dots to show that she was typing a message.

Just wanted to talk, that's all

Rough day at work? Abs sent back. She knew that a rough day at work for Hayley was going to be a lot worse than what most other people found themselves up against.

Yes, Hayley replied. There was a pause, and then another message came through. *Are you busy right now?*

Abs glanced up from her phone to look across the table. Logan had mostly turned her attention back to Sapphy, and they were having an intense conversation about some new programs they were looking at introducing, but Abs noticed that her gaze flickered over to check on her.

No

She typed the message out, and her thumb hovered over the send key as a little creeping sensation of guilt came over her. She felt bad for dipping out of the night like this, but she also didn't want Hayley to struggle with whatever had happened at work on her own.

Abs hit send before she could question her decision, watching the two little ticks appear beside her message.

I'm at home

"Where are you going?" Sapphy asked as Abs rose to her feet, stuffing her cell phone into the back pocket of her jeans. Logan and the others looked over too, noticing for the first time that something was up with her.

'The woman I sometimes secretly have sex with is having a shitty evening, so I'm bailing' didn't seem like a great response, even though it was an accurate one. Instead, Abs made up something about her mom needing help. They all knew about her injury, so they couldn't exactly get mad at her for rushing out to be with her.

It wasn't until she was in the back of her Uber on her way to Hayley's place, that Abs began to question just why she was feeling this sudden surge of urgency. Why had she dropped everything so quickly to rush out to Haley's side? This wasn't exactly the kind of support she could see herself extending to any other one (or two) night stand.

Abs rationalized it to herself as the Uber pulled into Hayley's street. She was just going there as a friend; this was a purely platonic gesture, the same as she'd do for Logan or any of her other friends. And besides, it wasn't like this was some kind of invitation to hook up; Gracie would be home.

That was what she told herself, over and over again, and when the Uber pulled up by Hayley's front door, Abs got out, checking which lights were on in the house as she did so. None of the lights on the first floor had been turned on, just the one in the front room.

Has Gracie already gone to bed, or was she downstairs with her mom?

When Abs knocked on the door, it took a little while longer than she had expected for Hayley to answer. She leaned in close to the door, listening out for any signs of life on the other side; the sound of movement slowly grew closer. The lock slid back before Hayley pulled the door open.

She looked awful.

Her skin was pale, almost gray in the harsh overhead light that illuminated the front porch. Her eyes were bloodshot, red rimmed and raw, like she'd been crying.

Something was wrong. Something was really *wrong.*

"Hey," Abs said quietly. She didn't really know what else to say—would she ask what had happened, or would she wait for Hayley to offer the story up?

"Hey." Hayley pulled the door open a little more and stepped back to let her inside. "Thanks for coming."

"It's okay." Abs kicked her shoes off, but as she did so, she realized Hayley was still wearing hers. She was still dressed in her work clothes, including her work lanyard. "Are you…alright?"

"You want a drink?" Hayley asked, as though she hadn't even spoken. Her voice was hollow, distant, like she was only half awake, and her gaze was oddly unfocused. She wasn't looking *at* Abs, rather she was looking past her, *through* her.

"I…sure." Abs glanced around, looking for any signs of Gracie in the house; her bag on the floor, her coat flung over the back of a chair, or maybe one of her school books on a table. There was nothing. "Is Gracie already asleep? It's kind of early."

"She isn't home." Hayley drifted into the front room, moving with a dreamlike quality, like she was just acting without really thinking about it. She dropped onto the couch, waiting for Abs to follow her. "I was supposed to work tonight, so she's at a friend's place."

"Supposed to be?" Abs sat down beside her gingerly. With every movement Hayley made, every word that came out with that same hollow, cold tone, she was getting more and more worried about her. "What happened?"

Hayley didn't answer her for a few moments, and again it felt like she hadn't really heard Abs. Instead, she just stared off into empty space.

"They sent me home," she said finally.

"Why?"

"Because…" Hayley stopped short of actually telling her. She inhaled slowly, deeply, like she was trying desperately to calm herself down, to ground herself. When she exhaled, it was shaky and nervous, as if her breath was catching on a lump somewhere in her throat. She closed her eyes for a moment and then hung her head.

90

She didn't answer straight away. Instead, she took a long swig from the glass in front of her. Abs wasn't sure what it contained, but she was fairly sure it wasn't water.

"It was a bad night," Hayley said finally, giving up nothing else.

"Do you want to talk about it?" Abs asked.

Abs couldn't help but feel as though she was way out of her depth here, trying to be a shoulder for Hayley to cry on. For most people she knew, a bad day at work meant a client had yelled at them, or perhaps they'd hurt themselves during a workout. She had no idea of how to even come to terms with the kind of horrors Hayley dealt with every day, let alone on a 'bad day'.

Without another word, Hayley straightened up, turned around, and leaned in to kiss Abs. She practically fell into her, grabbing her face with both hands, and taking Abs by surprise as she kissed her, hard. It was with the same kind of force and desperation as the first time they'd kissed. There was that same drive behind it, that same urgency.

Abs froze up, taken completely by surprise. This wasn't what she had expected at all. She was supposed to be there as a friend to Hayley, nothing more. She wasn't supposed to be kissing her, she wasn't supposed to be *here*, again. How did this keep happening to them?

Finally, after what felt like way too long, the rational part of Abs's brain kicked into gear, and she pushed Hayley away, gently but firmly. She kept the other woman at arm's length with a hand on her shoulder.

"What are you doing?" Hayley asked. She sounded hurt, borderline betrayed by Abs's rejection, and for the first time since she had opened the door, she actually looked focused, like she was really one hundred percent in the room with Abs.

"What are *you* doing?" Abs asked, frowning at her. This wasn't the Hayley that she'd come to know. This wasn't the rational, sensible woman who had told her over and over again that they should both keep their distance from each other.

"I just want to…" Hayley fumbled, searching for the right words without quite landing on them. "I just want to forget about work. Why do you think I called you?"

Why do you think I called you? That stung.

Abs didn't have much time to think about that though, because with those words, Hayley was leaning back in towards her, trying to kiss her again. This time though, Abs managed to anticipate the move and pulled away quickly.

She didn't want to though, not entirely. There was a selfish part of her brain that wanted nothing more than to just give in, to sink into the kiss, and then go upstairs to Hayley's bedroom to do what they had told themselves over and over again they would never repeat.

After all, Hayley had been the one to say that they should keep their distance from each other, and Abs was just respecting that. That was why Abs hadn't pushed things, that was why she had just kept things strictly professional between the two of them. Now that Hayley was practically throwing herself at her, giving her the green light to do whatever she wanted, it was a little harder to say no.

But still, there was that little voice in the back of her head, that glimmer of her subconscious which knew this was wrong. It was the voice that kept telling her to pull back from Hayley, to keep that distance between the two of them.

Deep down, she knew this wasn't a good idea. She knew this wasn't what Hayley really wanted. She was upset and angry and not at all in the right head space for any of this, and Abs knew that if anything happened between them tonight, she would just be taking advantage of how fragile Hayley was. If she ignored that little voice in the back of her head, Hayley would regret it in the morning, and she would probably end up resenting Abs.

"Is that the only reason you called me?" Abs asked quietly. "A quick fuck to make yourself feel better?"

Hayley couldn't quite meet her gaze. Her silence spoke volumes though, and Abs knew she was right. That was all this was to Hayley.She hadn't wanted comfort, or a shoulder to cry on. She'd just wanted something that Abs had already provided for her, nothing more.

It was surprising how much that realization stung. Was that really all she was good for in Hayley's eyes?

Abs's hands slid from Hayley's shoulders, and as they did, she hung her head again, covering her face with her hands. It was probably a good thing Gracie wasn't there with them, Abs figured. Hayley wouldn't have wanted her daughter to see her in this kind of state.

"Hayley..." She sighed heavily, trying her best to be as gentle as possible. "What happened tonight at work?"

"I don't want to talk about it," she said quietly, her voice muffled into the palms of her hands.

"Well, *I* didn't come here to fuck," Abs said, more coldly than she had intended. "So if that's all you called me here for, I'll see you around."

She got up to leave, but before she could even step away from the couch, Hayley's hand shot out and grabbed onto the sleeve of Abs's jacket. Her fingers curled into the fabric tightly. She looked up, meeting her gaze properly.

"Don't," she whispered. "Don't go. Please don't."

Thirteen

Hayley's eyes were wide with desperation as she clung to the sleeve of Abs's jacket. In that moment, she looked nothing like the mother who'd stormed into the gym to pry her daughter from the clutches of Abs and the other trainers. She was a shadow of the woman who had argued with Abs in her office, or the woman who'd slapped her. If anything, she looked more like a scared little girl than a grown woman.

As much as her comment about their relationship being little more than a few late night fucks had stung, Abs knew she couldn't just leave her there like that. She couldn't abandon her, not when she was clearly upset. So instead of storming out, Abs sank back down onto the couch beside her, waiting.

Was she going to explain what the hell was going on, or did she just not want to be alone?

Hayley relaxed her grip on Abs's sleeve, but didn't let go straight away. As she started to talk, her voice trembled, and Abs could tell that there were tears still clogging her throat.

"There was this call..." she began. "She was maybe a little younger than Gracie, I could hear it straight away. When adults call, they tend to know what information we're going to ask for, so they've got it at the ready. Kids are usually a little different. They know they're supposed to call us if they're in trouble, but they don't really know what information we need, especially when they're young. I could hear it in her voice, from the way she talked...she couldn't have been older than ten. And she was so...*so* scared."

She let go of Abs's sleeve, folding her hands into her lap. After a slow, shaky inhale, she kept going.

"I could hear yelling in the background. We get a lot of phone calls about domestic violence; a lot of scared kids who've hidden themselves away because Daddy's been

94

hitting Mommy again, and they don't know what to do. But this little girl, she told me that her dad had been drinking a lot, and her parents had started fighting. She'd gone to her room and was hiding there, but she said she was scared that he was going to come in there and hurt her, like he did to her mom."

Her voice started shaking so much that the words jumbled together, and she needed to take another second to steady herself. When she was ready, she carried on.

"She said that when they were fighting, her dad hit her mom. When she fell down, she smacked her head against the countertop, and she wasn't moving. Her older brother told her to go to her room, and she did, but...she was worried about her mom."

Hayley's head dropped into her hands for a third time, and her fingertips curled into the roots of her hair. Her breathing was raggedy, torn, and when she lifted her head again, Abs could see tears clinging to her lashes.

"I told her not to," she whispered, closing her eyes. "God, I *told her not to*, Abs. I told her to stay in her room and wait for the cops. They were on their way, they weren't far. But she was worried about her mom, and she wanted to try to check on her. I just heard yelling and screaming, and then I guess she dropped the phone and..."

There was a pause while Hayley wiped the tears from her cheeks. "The cops showed up, I heard them. The girl was okay, her brother too. They took her mom to hospital, I think. And the thing is, I've dealt with calls like that before. I've dealt with *worse* calls than that before. But that little girl, the yelling...how *terrified* she was..."

Abs had always wondered how people were able to do the kind of work that Hayley did without just breaking down into a thousand pieces. She'd always found it incredible that there were people out there who could listen to all that panic and misery, and still go home to their families at the end of their shift, as though nothing had happened.

The answer, as it turned out, was that sometimes they couldn't. Not when it hit too close to home, like this one obviously had.

"Did it remind you of Ed?" Abs asked.

Hayley huffed out a shaky sigh and nodded. Then she shook her head.

"He was never the one that yelled," she explained. "*I* was the one that yelled. When he got angry, he would never shout and scream, or throw things about like some drunks do. He just got...cold. He'd ice you out if you ever did anything wrong, make you feel like you didn't even exist. Make you *wish* you didn't even exist. That man I could hear on the phone was nothing like Ed was, but I guess it just...brought back what my life used to be. I just couldn't stop thinking about Gracie. What if she'd had to make that call one day?"

"But she didn't," Abs assured her gently. "You got out. Both of you did."

"Yeah, but...I just keep wishing things had turned out different." Hayley frowned, leaning back against the couch cushions. "I just keep wishing I'd gotten out sooner, so she never would have had to know him. Maybe that would be easier."

Abs's mom had felt the same way for a long time. It was something she'd only ever talked about when Abs was a little older, and able to understand everything that had happened, but it was something she would always remember. She could never forget how guilty her mom had felt about everything, even though none of it was her fault.

"What did you mean when you called yourself a 'formerly troubled kid'?"

"Hmm?" The question took Abs by surprise and pulled her out of her thoughts.

"The first time I came to the gym, that's what you said to me. 'One formerly troubled kid to the parent of a currently troubled kid', or something like that. What did you mean when you called yourself that?"

"Oh." Abs had kind of just figured that over the months, Hayley had just forgotten about that comment. After all, she had all but forgotten about it. "My dad. He was a lot like Ed is, and I guess when I looked at Gracie, I saw a lot of myself in her."

"Is that why you pushed so hard to keep her at the gym?"

"I suppose so," Abs mused, nodding her head slowly. She hadn't really thought about it that much at the time, but now it made some sense to her. "I think I remembered how shitty it was to feel like I had no one looking out for me when I was her age. I didn't want her to feel like she was completely alone for as long as I did."

"What was it like?" Hayley asked, her voice wavering with hesitation.

Abs knew why she was asking. It was a morbid, self-punishing curiosity that she couldn't quite quell. Abs knew that whatever she told Hayley about her dad would only end up being projected into whatever she imagined Ed was like with Gracie. She knew any stories she'd tell, like the time he got so drunk he forgot to pick her up from soccer practice after school, would only have Ed's face attached to them.

"It wasn't great," she admitted diplomatically.

Abs knew well enough just how badly it had torn her mom up to leave her alone with her father, so she had some idea of how guilty Hayley probably felt for leaving Gracie alone with Ed. She didn't want to add to that guilt by giving out all the gory details about her teenage years.

"Do you blame your mom?" Hayley's voice shook. "For what happened to you back then?"

"No." That was a no-brainer to Abs. The answer rolled off her tongue like a knee jerk response. "I don't blame her for any of it. She was just doing what she had to, doing whatever she could. Just like you've done with Gracie."

"I didn't want to give her up like that." Hayley began to pick at the hangnail on her left thumb, moving it in quick, nervous jerks. "I just thought it would be better for her, with the shifts I work. I knew I wouldn't be there if something happened to her during the night, and I knew that as shitty as Ed was—and I *did* know that he was a shitty parent—" Hayley shook her head. "I thought at least he'd be there. I knew it would never be good, but I just thought it would be *better*."

"She knows that, I think," Abs said quietly. She reached over and slipped her hand into Hayley's before she could tear the skin from her finger, then gave her hand a gentle squeeze. Her palm was clammy against Abs's, slick with sweat, but she didn't let go. She knew that this was what Hayley needed right now; a little human contact, a little comfort.

"You do?"

"Hmm." Abs nodded, looking down at their joined hands. "I talked to her about what it was like growing up with my dad, and she told me about Ed. And honestly, she didn't sound like she blamed you for any of this."

"No?" Hayley was hopeful; borderline desperate.

How long had this been nagging at the back of her mind for? Had she been worried about this since she'd first sent Gracie to live with Ed?

"She's a smart kid. I think she gets that this is all just a shitty situation. It's no-one's fault, you're just doing what you can."

"I guess so," Hayley said quietly, rubbing a hand over her face. "Suppose there's no point in going over it again and again like this. It won't change what's already happened."

"Exactly."

There was a beat of silence while Abs watched her, and Hayley just stared up at the ceiling blankly. She looked exhausted, and not the kind of exhaustion that came from after a long day of work. Those dark circles wouldn't fade after just a night of rest, and that lingering heaviness in her tone wouldn't go away after a weekend of fun.

She'd seen that same look on her mom's face, even years after her father had died. She knew there wasn't much she could do about it there and then, but she could help Hayley get a good night's sleep. At least that would be a start.

"C'mon," she said, standing up. "Let's get you into bed." After a moment of uncertainty, Hayley took the hand Abs offered out to her, and followed her up to her room. She stripped off slowly, tossing her clothes to the foot of her bed, and Abs found some pajamas for her to wear in the closet. She changed and sat down on the edge of her bed as Abs tidied her clothes into the laundry bin.

"You alright?" Abs asked, catching sight of her in the mirror above the dresser. Hayley frowned, shaking her head. "What's up?"

"I didn't mean what I said before."

She'd said a *lot* over the course of the evening. Abs tossed the last stray sock into the laundry bin and turned to face her. "Didn't mean what?"

"'Why do you think I called you over'?" Hayley quoted herself, frowning. "I didn't mean that. It was a shitty thing to say."

"It was," Abs agreed with a small smile. Hayley looked up at her, saw the smile, and returned it weakly.

"Sorry." She patted the bed beside her. Abs flicked the lid of the laundry bin closed and joined her on the comforter. "I don't even know why I said it. I didn't mean it."

"No?"

"No." She shook her head, looking up at Abs.

There was something different about the way she was looking at her now. The blind, wild desperation that Abs had seen when Hayley had tried to kiss her earlier, had gone. There wasn't the burning, almost angry passion that had been there when they'd first kissed either. It was something else, something she couldn't quite place.

"Then what am I?" Abs asked. "If I'm not just a late night fuck."

"I don't know yet. But I'd like to find out."

99

Abs knew it was the most honest answer Hayley could have given in that moment, and she believed her. She leaned in a little closer, and pressed her lips to Hayley's in a gentle, chaste kiss. It was nothing like the kisses they'd shared before; there was none of the urgency behind it. Hayley's lips still tasted like the last hints of her drink which Abs guessed had been vodka and the sharp bitterness seemed strange in contrast to the sweetness of the kiss.

Abs pulled back and stroked a stray strand of brown hair out of Hayley's eyes. "You feeling any better?"

"Yeah," she admitted. "But I don't want you to leave."

"I don't have to."

"I know, but..." Hayley paused. There was one catch, because of course there was. "Gracie. She's coming home tomorrow morning, around nine or ten."

"Then I'll set an alarm." Abs smiled. "Just let me clean up downstairs, and I'll be back up. If you want me to stay, then I'll stay."

Hayley didn't need convincing. She nodded eagerly, and Abs left her with a kiss on the forehead, before heading downstairs to clear up. She cleared away Hayley's glass, put her bag by the shoe rack where she'd seen it before, and checked that the doors were locked before heading back upstairs.

By the time she made it back into Hayley's room, she was asleep. She was curled on her side, her hands tucked neatly under her head. Abs could tell by her slow, steady breathing that she was out cold. She stripped off to her underwear slowly, taking care not to wake Hayley, before sliding into bed behind her, wrapping one arm loosely around her waist.

Yeah, this definitely wasn't the kind of treatment she'd offer up to any other one-night stand.

Fourteen

Neither one of them was quite sure of how to label whatever it was they had going on. It was obvious to both of them that it was something more serious than a one-night stand, or a friend with benefits relationship. But at the same time, it wasn't like Hayley was Abs's girlfriend. It wasn't like they went out on dates together, or were even open about their relationship. They were in a strange in-between stage that neither one really knew how to categorize, so they gave up trying to do so pretty quickly.

Instead, they just decided to make do with what it was that they had. They had agreed to take things slowly. Hayley was honest about the fact that she needed time, and Abs was more than happy to give it to her. More than anything, Hayley didn't want to upset or disrupt Gracie, and on more than one occasion she reminded Abs that her first priority would always be Gracie. So when she'd asked Abs if they could keep their distance from each other, to try to limit their contact when other people were around, Abs agreed.

After all, they had no idea if this would go anywhere anyway, and the upheaval it could cause in Gracie's life for what might be a few fumbles or a quick fling just didn't make sense. *No,* Abs assured herself, *keeping our distance from each other when others were around and protecting ourselves, as well as Gracie, emotionally, is the right thing to do.*

They still met up whenever they could. Hayley would send a text and Abs would jump at the chance to see her, to be with her. The sex was wild and wanton almost as if the sneaking about added to the thrill. But as the weeks went on, they both started to get a little more relaxed about that rule, and Abs began to find herself at Hayley and Gracie's place more and more often.

At first, she would just drive over when Gracie wasn't home. She'd go over on one of the evenings when she was at a friend's place, or during the day when Gracie was at school and Hayley didn't have a shift at work. And the more time she spent there, the less it became about the sex.

Of course, she'd be lying if she said that sex wasn't still a big and important part of it. But that wasn't *all* it was. Not anymore. They'd sit there together, huddled under the blankets as they traced invisible marks on each other's skin with the tips of their fingers, and in those stolen moments they had together, the rest of the world just seemed to melt away.

When Hayley drifted off beside her, the only sound Abs could hear was her breathing, which evened out and deepened as she fell asleep. The only thing she could smell was the faint perfume that was left over from her shampoo, and if she closed her eyes, she'd swear she could still taste Hayley's lips on her own. Nothing else mattered when they were together like that; any worries or responsibilities that were outside the house just faded away into nothing.

It was a good bit of fortune, as things turned out, that Abs and Gracie had become such good friends over the past few weeks, because when Hayley invited her over for dinner for the first time, Gracie was delighted. To her, it was just an innocent dinner with a family friend, nothing more than that. She never suspected anything else was going on between the two of them, and of course, why would she? They were discrete, at Hayley's request.

Abs had agreed to that condition. She'd agreed that it was probably for the best that they kept the truth about them a secret for the time being. She had told Hayley she was completely fine with keeping their relationship a secret until she was ready to come clean about everything, and she still stood by that. She wasn't going to ruin *whatever* it was that was going on between her and Hayley by pushing things too far, too fast.

But the more time the two of them spent around each other – whether it was in front of the other trainers at the gym, or at Hayley's place during those late night dinners with Gracie – the harder it became to pretend like there was nothing going on between the two of them. It was getting almost impossible to keep their interactions purely platonic, and Abs had a horrible feeling that sooner or later one of them was going to slip up. And knowing her luck, it was going to be her.

It would be all too easy, during one of those late night meals, to slip her arm around Hayley's waist or drop a kiss on her cheek. On more than one occasion, she'd caught herself staring at Hayley's ass during the middle of a workout, and she'd had to scold herself mentally. It wasn't her fault, she'd reasoned; it was all Hayley's fault for bending over in front of her while wearing *yoga pants*, for Christ's sake. She was only human, after all.

And although she was struggling just a bit with maintaining her professional composure all the time, Abs figured that they weren't making it *too* obvious to the outside world that something was going on. Sure, they were obviously getting along a lot better than they had been before, but given the way their first couple of meetings had gone, that wasn't exactly hard.

Of course, Abs hadn't exactly counted on Sapphy being as intuitive as she was. Sapphy could tell when Abs's hand was hurting just from the way she held her coffee cup. Back in college, she had known that Abs was about to break up with her first serious girlfriend, probably before Abs even did. It was kind of like a weird sixth sense twins sometimes claimed to have, but it only went one way.

Given all that, it was pretty stupid of Abs to go about her life believing that Sapphy wouldn't pick up on *something* strange going on between her and Hayley. When the initial 'slap' had happened in the gym, Sapphy had known about it within the hour. Logan swore it wasn't her that had told her,

103

but Sapphy had a weird way of always knowing what was happening at all times.

As the weeks went by, and Abs found herself spending more and more time with Hayley, she began to notice out of the corner of her eye that Sapphy was looking at them more frequently, glancing over at them every so often from the other side of the gym, or looking down from her office. Soon enough, she seemed to zero in on them whenever Hayley would come in for a class. She suspected something was up, but she had no way of actually proving it.

"You two are getting along well," she commented one evening, once Hayley had left the gym after one of their classes together.

Abs was clearing up some equipment they'd used back into the cupboard, with her back to her friend. It was a good thing she wasn't looking at Sapphy, or else her friend might have seen the shock on her face.

"Who two?" She feigned ignorance for a moment, but she caught sight of Sapphy's expression and backpedaled. "Yeah, I guess we are."

"When did that happen?"

Abs shrugged in what she hoped was a nonchalant gesture. "I don't really know. I guess I just won her over with my charming personality."

"Uh huh…" Sapphy didn't sound very convinced by her excuse. "It's just weird."

"You don't think I can make friends? Am I really that annoying?" Abs dusted off her hands, locked up the cupboard, and turned to face her best friend. "I'm a little insulted, but okay. We'll move past it."

Sapphy narrowed her eyes for a moment, before just outright saying what was on her mind. "Is there something going on between the two of you?"

Oh shit.

She had to just be guessing, right? Surely she was just throwing the idea out there, because there was no real way she could know for sure. Right?

"What makes you say that?"

Sapphy shrugged. "I don't know. Is there?"

"No."

Abs had never lied to her best friend before. Well, she *had* lied, but up until that moment, they had only ever been little white lies that never meant anything in the grand scheme of things. No, her hand wasn't hurting her; no, she wasn't jealous of Sapphy's spur of the moment romantic getaway to Mexico; yes, she loved that new haircut.

She'd never lied about something that actually *mattered* though. Relationships were just one of those things that they tended to share loads of exciting details about with each other. Before her relationship with Hayley, she'd never felt the need to keep something like that from Sapphy. She'd never had a reason to. But now, things were different.

The lie came out so quickly and naturally that Abs was surprised in herself and instantly felt a pang of guilt. When the truth came out, *if* it came out, then Sapphy would be pissed and rightfully so.

"Okay." Sapphy shrugged, as if that settled things completely for her. "I was just curious."

And with that, the conversation was over. She didn't have any more questions, she didn't need to hear anything else from Abs. And that only made her feel worse. Sapphy trusted her to tell the truth, she trusted her to be honest about these kinds of things.

Maybe if she ever actually came clean about it, Logan would understand why they'd lied. *Hopefully* she would.

Abs shot her friend a weak smile, before making some excuse about paperwork that allowed her to escape up to her office for some peace. Maybe she would be able to talk to Hayley about this secrecy? After all, it had to be weighing on her just as much. She couldn't be enjoying sneaking around and lying like this.

Thankfully, her phone lit up on her desk, offering up a distraction for her. She picked it up and surprisingly, she saw a message from Hayley on the home screen.

Gracie went to a friend's house. Want to come over?

She was already typing out 'yes' before she'd even really finished reading the message. It was truly just a bit shameful how quick she was to jump at the chance to see Hayley, even for a little while, but Abs didn't care that much.

Abs didn't have that much time left on the clock for her shift, and she wasn't really in the mood to face Sapphy again after the conversation the two of them had had, so she decided to leave early and go see Hayley. Perhaps they could talk about this, or maybe they could figure out what their next few steps were going to be.

She gathered up her things and headed out of the gym quickly, ducking around Logan before she got caught up in a conversation with her. Once she was out of the gym, she headed to her car, got in, and drove straight to Hayley's place.

Fifteen

"What are you thinking about?" Abs asked.

They were curled up together on the couch in Hayley's front room, with the remnants of the evening scattered about them. Abs's jacket was on the floor of the entryway by her shoes, where Hayley had all but ripped it off her when she'd come in. There were two glasses and an empty bottle of wine on the coffee table.

The TV was on low, giving off that empty gray static noise that Abs was more than happy to let just wash over her. Some crappy B movie she'd never heard of before was playing; they'd switched it on to give themselves some background noise initially, but now Hayley was staring blankly at the screen.

"Hmm?" she murmured. "What was that?"

"What are you thinking about?" Abs repeated, pressing a kiss to her shoulder. Hayley stirred, rolling over so that she was facing Abs.

"I'm thinking…" she began, reaching up to brush a strand of blonde hair back from Abs's forehead. "I'm thinking that this is nice. I like being here with you, just like this."

Abs grinned. Hayley's face was still cast mostly in shadow since neither of them had bothered to turn on the lights when she'd come in, but the weak glow from the TV danced over her features, softening them. She looked beautiful.

"I like being here, too."

Hayley's smile faded quickly though, and she lowered her gaze, looking down. She pulled her lower lip between her teeth, worrying the skin, and then when she looked up again, with a frown.

"Can I ask you something?" she whispered.

"Of course."

"You're the first woman I've been with," she admitted. "*Ever*."

"Really?" Abs cocked an eyebrow. "Huh…"

"What?" Hayley lifted her head up quickly, suddenly panicked. "What's wrong?"

"Nothing, I just…figured, you had more experience. I mean, you sure seemed to know what you were doing when you—"

"Oh, shut up." She dropped her head back down onto the couch cushions, cuddling up to Abs. For a moment she was quiet, and then when she spoke again, her voice was muffled into Abs's neck. "It's really not a problem?"

"Why would it be?"

"Dunno." She shrugged, a little awkwardly. "I know some people don't like women who've…been with men."

"I sort of figured you'd been with a man before," Abs reminded her, wrapping an arm around her shoulder. "Having met your kid and ex-husband and all."

"You know what I mean. I didn't want you to think I was…" Hayley paused, searching for the right way to get out how she was feeling, before giving up with a sigh. Her head was foggy after half a bottle of red wine and a long week at work, and she was far too tired to traverse the inner politics of what little exposure she'd had of the lesbian community. "Oh, I don't know. You know what I mean though, right?"

"I know what you mean, don't worry."

Outside, it had started raining. The first few light drops scattered against the windowpane, and then gradually began to get heavier. Abs closed her eyes as she listened to the rainfall against the glass, drumming out a steady beat.

"I think I've always known," Hayley continued, her voice quiet.

"Always?"

"I just never did anything about it. I never had any friends who were gay when I was growing up, and I guess I thought if I just ignored it for long enough, then it would go away."

"Is that why you ended up with Ed?"

"Yes," she whispered. "He was popular, good-looking. All the girls were crazy about him, and I think because I just wanted to fit in back then, I acted like I was too. And then when he asked me out for the first time, I said yes. I don't know why. And then..."

Her voice faded into silence. She sighed heavily.

"I blamed it on a lot of different things. My job, the fact that we had a baby, the drinking, the other women. It was all those things, but it was me too. I was the problem too, I guess I was just too afraid to admit it."

"That must have been hard," Abs said quietly, stroking her hand up and down Hayley's arm soothingly.

Abs had never had the painful, traumatic coming out experience that so many of her friends had struggled with. Her mom was always supportive of her, and when Abs had brought her first girlfriend home, it didn't seem like it had been that much of a shock to her. Even her father, for all his faults, would never have had a problem with her. But she knew that sometimes, coming out was much more difficult than it had been for her. Sometimes it was too difficult to even admit to yourself, let alone the people around you.

"I just kept pushing it down, over and over," Hayley murmured. "All my friends keep pushing me to date again, now that Gracie is a little older. They keep trying to set me up with their coworkers, or cousins, and I just keep turning them down, but none of them know why. I remember when one of my friends set me up on a dating app, they make you put your gender preference in when you set up your profile, and I just *froze*. Clicking on 'men' just felt so wrong, but I couldn't bring myself to click on 'women', or even 'both'."

"You don't think they'd support you?"

"No, I know they would," she admitted with a sigh. "I know they'd stand by me no matter what, but after all this time...I don't know. It's confusing."

"I know."

"When did you come out?" Hayley asked.

"You looking for tips?" Abs joked, without opening her eyes. She felt Hayley slap her arm gently and smiled at the light touch. "I don't think I ever did. I just came home one day with a girl and my mom was just like 'Yeah, this checks out'. Then she probably baked something for us."

"Sounds nice."

"I'll bet it was. My mom's a good cook."

"Gracie told me that," Hayley admitted. "She actually told me a lot about you once I started coming to classes."

"Oh, really? What'd she tell you?"

"All bad things," Hayley murmured, nuzzling into Abs's neck. The tip of her nose was cold against Abs's skin, but her lips were warm when she pressed a soft kiss there. "All very bad."

"Ah, all true then."

She felt Hayley's lips pull back into a smile against her neck as she nodded. "All true."

For a few moments they fell silent, just listening to the rain outside, and Abs thought Hayley had fallen asleep beside her, but then she spoke again.

"I don't know how to tell her about us."

Gracie. She must have been talking about Gracie. Abs had never dated anyone with kids before, so this was new territory for her. The closest she'd ever come was a woman who was concerningly attached to her pug, but she sort of figured that wasn't the same thing.

"There's no rush," Abs assured her. "I get it, you want to take things slow."

"I just..." Hayley paused. "Things are going really well right now. She's doing better in school, she's hanging out with her friends more often. She seems happier, just...*better*, and I don't want things to change. She even agreed to go to regular meetings with a guidance counselor to help get her GPA up, and she was talking about college last night. I don't want to...disrupt her."

Yeah, this wasn't in the same ballpark as the girlfriend with the pug.

"Then we don't have to tell her." Abs wrapped her arm around Hayley a little more tightly, smiling. "We don't have to do anything. I'm fine with the way things are right now."

"You are?" Hayley lifted her head. "You're not mad?"

"How could I be mad?" Abs smiled, turning her head a little so she could meet Hayley's gaze. "Like I said, I like being here with you like this. And if I've got to keep it a secret in order to keep doing that, then that's what I'll do."

Hayley beamed up at her before tucking her head back in towards Abs's chest again, cuddling up to her. "Thanks."

"It's okay," she whispered, feeling another pang of guilt somewhere deep in her gut, which she tried to push down.

Abs really wanted to talk to Hayley about coming clean and starting to be more open about their relationship. At the very least, she wanted to try to figure out just what this actually was. But after seeing Hayley's face, and realizing how relieved she was that she didn't have to worry about going public too quickly, Abs knew it wasn't the right time.

There would be other chances to talk about it, she told herself. Maybe after a few more weeks Hayley would feel more comfortable with the idea of actually 'coming out' and telling people about their relationship. But right now, it was clear she wasn't at that point, and Abs was determined to stick to her promise. She wasn't going to force Hayley into something she didn't want to do.

111

Sixteen

One night, while Gracie was at a friend's house so that the two of them could spend an evening together, Abs found out why Hayley had become an emergency dispatcher in the first place. It was during those stolen hours after sunset that she truly felt like she was getting to know this woman. It was like the longer they spent together, the more layers of Hayley were peeled back. First, she was the hard-ass mother, then she was that nervous, uncertain woman who Abs had first slept with. And now she was…something else entirely. Abs didn't even know how to describe her anymore.

Abs found herself longing for those evenings together, once the house was quiet. They would dim the lights, pull out a bottle of wine to share between the two of them, curl up together under a blanket, and just talk for hours. Then one evening, late at night while they were both drifting off to sleep, she asked the question that had been at the back of her mind for months.

"Why a 911 operator?"

"Huh?" Hayley lifted her head from where it was resting on Abs's shoulder.

"Why a 911 operator?" she repeated. In her mind, it was impossible to picture actively pursuing a career where she would have to listen to people at their lowest, at their worst. And yet, here Hayley was in front of her, doing exactly that.

"I could say the same thing about your job." Hayley laughed.

"Well, to be fair, I became a gym trainer because I was a good boxer."

"And I'm a good listener?"

"So is that why you decided to become a dispatcher?"

"No," Hayley admitted, smiling gently. "That isn't why."

"Then why *did* you?"

Hayley tilted her head to one side, as if she was only now considering it for the first time. "You know, I went through that whole phase when I was a little kid where I wanted to be a cop, a doctor, and a firefighter...probably all at once, actually. But I think back then it was all just make believe, you know? I didn't really understand what people in those jobs did, I just had this vague idea of what they did; of 'helping' people. But back then, I think that was all I knew. When I was about eleven or twelve, my grandma had a heart attack. It wasn't a major one, and she lived for like fifteen years afterwards, but I was the only one there at the time, so I was the one who made the 911 call."

She paused for a few moments, staring off into the middle distance as if she could see the whole thing unfolding in front of her eyes again. "I don't really remember much about that day, to be honest, but I *do* remember panicking, being so scared that I could barely even get my grandma's address out. And then I heard this voice on the other end of the line..."

"911, what's your emergency?" Abs quoted, smiling. She'd heard it enough times on TV to know it by heart.

"That's the one." Hayley chuckled. "And you know, I was absolutely terrified. I was in this completely crazy situation for a kid to be in, but that guy on the other end of the line was so calm, it just made it so much easier. I felt less scared because of that guy, and I was able to be there for my grandma. And I think ever since then, I've wanted to be able to do that for someone else. For another little kid. It's kind of silly, I guess."

"It's not." Abs yawned, cuddling up to her. "It's as good a reason as any to start a job."

"Are you falling asleep on me?" Hayley asked, gently poking her in the side.

"Yeah." Abs didn't even bother pretending that she wasn't tired. "When's Gracie getting back?"

"Probably about ten or eleven?"

113

"Hmm…" Abs hummed, wrapping an arm around Hayley as she buried herself even further under the comforter. "We'll be up before then."

Hayley probably said something else to her. Maybe just *goodnight*, but if she did, then Abs didn't notice. She was already fast asleep.

<hr>

* * *

Abs woke up to the sound of people yelling. At first, she wasn't quite sure what they were yelling about, she just knew that they were angry about *something*.

"Mom, what the *fuck*?!"

"Gracie!"

Abs opened her eyes, blinking away sleep. She was still in Hayley's bed. Sunlight was pouring through the open curtains. The alarm clock on the bedside table showed that it had just gone to eight.

And Gracie was standing in the doorway to Hayley's room.

Oh shit.

"Gracie—" She scrambled up, pulling the covers around herself with no idea of what to say. "Gracie, wait, listen—"

"I cannot *believe* this shit!" Gracie yelled, taking a step backwards from Hayley, who was already on her feet. "Don't *touch* me!"

"Gracie, please just listen to me," Hayley begged. She was only in a dressing gown, which she must have grabbed when Gracie came in.

Shit, did Gracie come home early? She must have done. Abs's brain was struggling to catch up.

114

"Stay away from me, Mom!" Gracie yelled, running from the doorway. Hayley followed close behind her, calling her name, which gave Abs a chance to pull on her clothes.

She threw her clothes on and headed out into the upstairs hall, only to come face to face with another teenage girl. "Who are you?"

"I'm...Gracie's friend. Molly?"

"Great. Where'd Gracie go?" Abs asked. She and Hayley were nowhere to be seen, but downstairs, she heard the front door slam. "Shit."

As fast as she ran, by the time she made it to the door, Gracie had already disappeared. Hayley obviously couldn't chase her out into the street in just a dressing gown. When Abs made it outside, she had no idea which direction the teenager had even run in.

Abs rushed back inside the house, just as Molly was making her way down the stairs. "Did Gracie go?"

"She ran off, I don't even know which way she went." Abs ran a hand through her hair, trying to think. If *she* was a pissed off teenager, where would she run to? "Do you have any idea where she'd go?"

Molly just shrugged listlessly. "I dunno."

Fantastic.

"Alright. Where do you live? Do you live far from here?"

"A couple of blocks away. Like...a ten-minute walk, maybe."

"Good. Go home, right now. If Gracie shows up to your house, call Hayley." Abs pointed her in the direction of the door and didn't even wait for her to leave before she headed upstairs to look for Hayley. She found her in her bedroom, practically tearing clothes out of her closet to wear.

"Gracie. Oh God...oh God, oh God..." she whispered to herself, tugging on a sweater. There were tears rolling down her cheeks, frustrated, angry tears. As she caught sight of Abs in the doorway, she froze.

115

"It's alright," Abs said, even though she didn't *feel* alright. Her heart was pounding, her hands were shaking, and her legs felt like she'd run a marathon. "We'll find her. She can't have gone far. I sent that girl Molly home to wait for her, and we can go—"

"Go where?" Hayley yelled. "Where would she go? How the hell would you *know* where she's gone?"

Abs swallowed nervously. "I don't know. But we'll find her, okay? We can look at the gym, and at her dad's place, and maybe at the bowling alley…"

"Why the *fuck* would she have gone to the bowling alley?!" Hayley yelled. "Jesus *Christ*…if anything happens to her…I swear I'll…"

She was practically hyperventilating now. Tears were flooding down her cheeks, and she was breathing so hard that she could hardly speak. She was panicking, and that wasn't going to help them find Gracie.

"Hayley, try to breathe," Abs said gently, reaching out a hand to touch her shoulder. She smacked Abs's hand away though, taking a step backwards.

"This wouldn't have happened if she'd never gone to that damned gym. I'd never have met you, Gracie would be safe. Fuck!" she spat, before pushing past her to get to the hallway. "I wish I'd never met you."

Abs reeled backwards at the words. *She wished she never met me?*

Hayley didn't mean it. Of course she didn't mean it, she was just angry. Or at least, that was what Abs told herself when she followed Hayley out of the bedroom and to the hallway. She was just lashing out.

But as Abs got downstairs, she caught sight of Hayley's expression, and then she just wasn't so sure. She'd seen Hayley in a lot of different moods. She'd seen her irritated, she'd seen her determined, she'd seen her downright furious, but this was something completely different. When Hayley met her gaze, there was just pure unbridled anger in her eyes.

"Do you..." Abs cleared her throat. "We can take my car and start looking for her."

Hayley didn't even bother responding. She just turned on her heel and walked out of the house, snatching her keys up as she went. Abs followed behind her, and as soon as they had gotten into the car, Hayley began calling around. She must have gone through every other number on her phone to get a hold of someone who had seen Gracie, but every phone call ended the same way. She always hung up with a quiet 'please call me if you hear anything' before moving onto the next person in her contact list.

Abs had her eyes on the road the whole time. Or more accurately, she had her eyes on the sidewalk, looking for Gracie. She nearly pulled over a couple of times, after spotting a teenager who looked something like the girl they were searching for, but both times it was a stranger.

She wasn't sure how long they'd been out there looking for Gracie when Hayley's phone rang, startling them both. She was so desperate to pick up the phone that she answered without even bothering to check the caller ID. "Hello? Gracie? Is that you, honey?"

Abs pulled up to the side of the road as Hayley listened to whoever was on the other end of the line. She couldn't make out whatever it was they were saying, but she had a feeling that it wasn't Gracie calling. Hayley's face was frozen in a mixture of shock and confusion, and after a few moments of listening to the other person talk, she just asked, "When?"

The other person on the line spoke again, and then Hayley hung up. Blood seemed to have drained from her face as she sat there, slowly bringing the phone away from her ear. Her mouth opened just a little, as if she was about to speak, but nothing came out.

"Hayley?" Abs leaned over, touching her shoulder gently. "Hayley, what is it? Who called you?"

"It was the hospital." Hayley's voice came out barely above a whisper, and even though Abs sat only a few inches from her, she struggled to hear her. "They…she got hit by a car. She's in ICU."

Seventeen

"She's going to be okay," Abs said quietly, tightening her grip on the steering wheel a little more. She wasn't sure whether she was assuring herself or Hayley more, she just knew that she didn't really sound all that confident. Her voice was wavering, shaking with nerves.

Hayley sat beside her in the passenger's seat, staring straight ahead blankly. Her eyes were glassy and unfocused, but rimmed pink from unshed tears.

"You don't know that," Hayley said quietly.

It would be alright. It had to be alright, Gracie had to be okay. People didn't run into the street and get hit by cars. People didn't die from freak accidents like that. It was just something you heard about on the news, or saw in movies. It didn't happen in real life.

"Gracie is going to be fine, Hayley," she repeated, tapping her fingers against the steering wheel over and over. "She's going to be fine."

Hayley didn't say anything back. She just kept staring straight ahead with that same blank, lifeless stare, as if Abs wasn't even in the car with her. She didn't say anything, not even after they'd parked in the hospital parking lot and gone inside. Abs had to ask for the room number, because when Hayley opened her mouth, nothing came out.

They rode the elevator up together in silence, beside a young guy holding a bunch of flowers and a kid in a wheelchair who was playing on her phone. ICU was on the third floor, and as Abs watched the numbers tick up, she began to feel sick.

"Third floor."

The calm voice of the announcer did nothing to make Abs feel better, and as the elevator came to a halt, she almost wished that the doors could stay closed. She wished she could just keep riding the elevator up, just so she wouldn't have to get out and see Gracie like that. She knew what people looked like when they were in ICU. They had wires sticking out of them, oxygen masks covering their faces, and drips pumping them full of fluid to keep them alive.

The doors opened though, just like they were supposed to.

Abs inhaled slowly, trying to steady herself as she stepped out of the elevator. She had to keep it together, for Hayley's sake if nothing else. She had to get her to Gracie's room, she had to make sure she had someone there for her; a shoulder to lean on.

The two stepped out onto the third floor. To the right was the nurse's station, to the left were the double doors that led into the ward. The name of the ward loomed overhead in big blue letters.

INTENSIVE CARE UNIT

Intensive care. That sounded so much worse than ICU. It made it sound *real*. There was nowhere to hide from how sick Gracie was now, not with that name hanging over them.

Hayley slipped her hand into Abs's. It was the first time she'd even touched her since they'd been caught by Gracie, and she was clinging onto Abs so tightly that it almost hurt. Her fingers tangled into Abs's, wrapping around them until her knuckles were white with the strain, but Abs didn't pull away. She couldn't bring herself to do it.

It was what Hayley needed right there and then.

Hayley probably still hated Abs a little, for everything that had happened. She probably saw Abs as being just a little responsible for what had happened to her daughter, and there was a horrible sinking sensation right in the pit of Abs's stomach that when all this was over, Hayley was going to want nothing more to do with her. The least she could do before that happened was to just be there for her, however she could.

The doors to ICU swung open to greet them automatically as they made their way to the nurses' station. They were asked to wait for just a few moments so the doctor could speak to Hayley, and the nurse indicated towards seats on the opposite wall.

"She is stable." The nurse placed her hand on Hayley's arm. "The doctor won't be a moment."

"I just want to see her. I need to see her," Hayley pleaded and before the nurse could respond a tall, thin man in scrubs and a white coat appeared behind the nurse.

"Mrs. Spencer?" he asked, dipping his head to meet her eyes.

"Yes—no, I mean, my name is Campbell, Hayley Campbell, I div—" Hayley shook her head. "Sorry, I'm Gracie's mom. How is she? Is she okay? Can I see her?"

"Let's take a seat." The doctor placed his hand on Hayley's arm, leading her gently to the chairs which the nurse had indicated to earlier. Abs followed.

Oh my God, she needed to sit down for this...

"Hayley, I'm Dr. Medway. I'll be treating Gracie now that she has been transferred to ICU. Now, the good news is that she has been deemed well enough to be transferred from ER to ICU. She is breathing on her own, however..." The doctor paused and took a breath while he seemed to consider his words. "Gracie has suffered quite a severe concussion. A CT scan suggests there has been some swelling to the brain, as well as an increase in fluid."

"Oh God." Hayley's eyes widened, her hand flew up to cover her mouth. Abs came around beside her and squeezed her shoulder.

"The good news is that there is no bleeding, but for the moment, Gracie isn't conscious. Now that is understandable at this point. Consider it the body's way of allowing itself time to heal." He paused once again, almost checking to see if any of his words were being absorbed by Hayley. "We'll be monitoring her condition to ensure the swelling does

121

reduce and there are no complications, but what we don't know is how long that'll take."

Hayley was nodding, but Abs could see the tears well up in her eyes. The doctor talked a little more about scans and wouldn't be drawn on Hayley's questions about when Gracie might wake up or, God forbid, what if she didn't?

It's a waiting game, he had explained. Yet, it didn't feel like a game at all.

* * *

Gracie's room was towards the back of the ward. The nurse they had seen earlier led them down the long corridor past a series of closed doors. With each door they passed, Abs felt worse and worse. She couldn't imagine what Hayley must be feeling.

She'd spent enough time in hospitals over the years to know the sound of them. There was a pretty consistent low buzz that permeated the air whenever you set foot in a hospital, a reminder that somewhere around you, someone was hard at work. Nurses were moving around, organizing charts and checking medication. Doctors were bustling around the corridors, anxious family members were tapping their feet against the tiled floor and pacing the waiting area. All of that energy, the nerves and excitement and fear that normally filled the air in a hospital, all of that was to be expected.

But in the ICU, there was none of that.

Deep down, Abs knew that it was ridiculous to think like this. She could still hear people moving around the ward, she could still hear nurses talking amongst themselves, and as they passed by a door that was ajar, they heard the steady beep of a heart rate monitor. There were still sounds all around her. But still, it felt wrong. It felt so different to every other ward in every other hospital.

The silence here was different. It was too quiet, too sterile. There was only one way to describe the surrounding silence, but as they approached Gracie's room, she didn't want to let her mind go there.

Hayley's breath caught in her throat when they came to a stop outside Gracie's room, and her grip on Abs's hand tightened until she was sure the circulation was being cut off. When Abs looked at her, she saw fresh tears in her eyes threatening to spill over, and a fresh wave of guilt flooded over her.

"I don't know if I can go in there." Hayley's voice quivered as she spoke. "I don't...I can't see her like that."

What was Abs supposed to say to her? Was she supposed to goad her into opening the door, or tug on her heartstrings and guilt her into doing it? She'd never been in this position before, she'd never had to think about anything that even came close to this.

"I'm right here," she whispered. "You don't have to do this alone. I'm going to be right here beside you."

Hayley turned her head, just a little, to look at Abs. Her eyes were wide, desperate and terrified like a child, and for a moment Abs thought she would just break down into uncontrollable tears right there and then. She wouldn't have blamed her if she did.

"Please don't leave."

A selfish wave of relief washed over Abs at those words. A part of her had still been worried that Hayley had really meant what she'd said before; she truly wished they'd never met, and Abs was the worst thing to happen to her.

"I'm not going anywhere," she promised Hayley, managing a weak smile for her benefit. "I'll be right here beside you, okay?"

"Okay." Hayley nodded, taking a moment to mentally steel herself.

Abs couldn't imagine the kind of mess her head was right now; hell, she was struggling to cope with the emotional roller-coaster of the last few hours. The kind of pain Hayley was going through was unimaginable.

As the nurse swung the door open to Gracie's room, Hayley seemed glued to the spot, transfixed by the sight of her daughter lying on the hospital bed. Abs felt Hayley's grip on her hand tighten again, and if she'd been paying a little more attention, Abs probably would have winced from the pain, but it just didn't register for her.

"Gracie…" Hayley whimpered, stumbling into the room and dragging Abs along with her. "Oh God…"

It was real, Abs realized. Gracie was really there, in that hospital bed. She was really hooked up to all those machines and monitors. This wasn't a movie or an anonymous story on the internet, it was real and it was happening in front of her.

"She looks so small," Hayley croaked, dropping Abs's hand as she rushed to the bed. She reached out to touch Gracie's cheek, but hovered over her face without making contact, just for a few seconds. It was like she was afraid if she actually touched her skin, Gracie would shatter beneath her fingertips like fine glass. "So fragile."

Abs couldn't breathe. It felt like someone was standing on her chest, crushing her lungs and squeezing all the air out. She just couldn't believe that was really *Gracie* in front of her. There was a dressing over part of her head, which came over the left side of her forehead. Several IV drips surrounded the bed. Abs remembered the doctor had said something about medications to reduce the swelling and reduce fluid, but the sight of Gracie lying helpless seemed to make the words swirl around her head in a jumble.

The nurse explained something about it looking worse than it was, but Hayley wasn't listening; she was at Gracie's bedside, holding her hand. It was only at that point Abs realized Gracie's other arm was in a cast. Hayley was right, she really did look fragile, and right now, as Hayley stood next to her daughter's bedside, so did Hayley.

"Here." Abs grabbed a heavy, wood framed seat with vinyl cushions and pushed it towards where Hayley stood. "Sit down."

Hayley pulled it closer and sat down, still clutching onto her daughter's hand, then she brought it up to her lips as if her breath might waken her. Abs pulled up a harder plastic chair and sat alongside Hayley when the nurse left, simply stroking her back, letting her know she was there for her. Neither of them said a word.

It seemed like they had been sitting like that for an hour or two when Hayley's phone buzzed in her pocket. She pulled it out to check who was calling. Abs assumed it was one of her friends, calling to ask if she'd heard any more news, but when her face collapsed into a look of disgust, she realized it couldn't have been.

"You okay?" she asked quietly.

"It's Ed," Hayley murmured, frowning down at her phone screen. "The hospital must have called him. I'll be back in a minute."

She excused herself to take the call out in the hallway, leaving Abs alone with Gracie. Hayley was right, with wires and tubes sticking out of her like this, surrounded by all these huge, imposing monitors, she really did look fragile.

It wasn't as bad as it could have been, Abs told herself sternly. After all, Gracie had been hit by a car; she could have been in a full body cast, or paralyzed, or—no.

Abs wasn't going to think like that.

That didn't happen in real life, remember?

She slowly approached Gracie's bed, shuffling her feet along the tiled floor until she was right by her bedside, where Hayley had stood just a few moments earlier. Here, she could see the scratches that covered Gracie's face, the scrape on her forehead, and the cut on her lower lip. She could see the cast

125

they'd put her right arm into, and the bruises that were blossoming over her skin.

It could be worse.

It could be worse.

She tried to tell herself that over and over again, but with each attempt it got a little harder. Sure, it *could* have been so much worse, but that didn't make this any better. It didn't make it any easier to look at the steady blip of the heart rate monitor beside her bed, or the oxygen saturation levels, or the screens of all the other machines that she didn't understand.

With trembling fingers, Abs reached out to touch Gracie's hand, gently resting the tips of her fingers against her knuckles.

"I'm so sorry, Gracie," she whispered. She wasn't even sure what she was apologizing for at this point. She just knew that she felt guilty.

They shouldn't have carried on the relationship for as long as they did. They should have cut things off at the start, right after they slept together for the first time, like Hayley had suggested. They should have kept their distance, kept things completely professional. Fuck, maybe she shouldn't have even pushed for Gracie to keep coming to classes at the gym. Maybe she should have just left well enough alone, rather than pushing her nose into their family. At least that way none of this would have happened.

The door opened behind her, and Abs turned to see Hayley returning. The skin around her eyes was blotchy and her nose was red. She'd been crying.

"Are you okay?" Abs asked.

"Ed," was all she said, shaking her head slowly. "Fucking *asshole.*"

"What did he say?"

Hayley just shook her head tersely, worrying her lower lip between her teeth until she tore the skin. She didn't want to talk about it, and given that Abs was treading on thin ice around her anyway, she didn't want to push the matter.

The two of them sat there for a while in silence. Abs wasn't sure how much time passed, but it felt like her back was melding into the chair. It was hard to tell with the blinds drawn, but a nurse came in to change Gracie's IV at some point, so they must have been there for a while. The nurse explained Gracie's next CT scan had been scheduled for first thing in the morning and suggested they go home and get some rest.

"Hayley, why don't I take you home to pick up some things for Gracie?" Abs suggested. Hayley didn't say anything, but she nodded slowly.

Eighteen

When they finally left and made their way back into the parking lot, there wasn't another soul around. The drive back was silent too. It was so silent that Abs could hear the air whipping around her car, and she could almost hear the gears working away in the engine too. It was a horrible, cold silence. The longer it went on, the more unbearable it became. But she couldn't quite bring herself to break it.

She tried putting on the radio just for a little background noise, but even that didn't work. They were too loud, too excited, too happy to be there. It all just felt *wrong*. She turned it off again, and the hyperactive late night radio show hosts faded back into the airwaves. They drove the rest of the way back in silence until she pulled into the same space on Hayley's street where she always did, and put the car in park. Between dropping Gracie off after class and sneaking here to meet Hayley when she was alone, she'd been there so many times before, but this time felt different.

An uncomfortable, heavy silence settled between the two of them as they sat there for a few minutes, without even the radio for some company. Hayley was looking down at her lap, fiddling with her keys, and Abs was looking straight ahead, unable to meet her gaze.

"I didn't mean what I said before," Hayley said, finally breaking the silence.

"Huh?" Abs looked at her quickly, taken by surprise.

"I didn't mean any of it," Hayley repeated. "All that crap I said before, about wishing I'd never met you. I didn't mean any of it."

Abs focused straight ahead at the first splatter of rain against her windshield. That was easier, she figured, than meeting Hayley's gaze. Even if she wasn't pissed anymore, even if she wasn't angry and hurt and lashing out at Abs, she still didn't want to look at her. Because what if she looked at her and that anger was still there in her eyes?

"Abs," Hayley whispered her name and reached out across the car. She laid her hand over Abs's, where it was still resting on the steering wheel. "Please look at me."

The rain was starting to pick up speed now, falling with steadier, heavier drops against the windshield. The streetlights outside were speckled and blurred from the water, distorting the world around them until it all just faded into a fuzzy mess of color. The only thing in focus now was Hayley and her hand, which was folded over Abs's.

Finally, she managed to look over at her.

The anger she'd seen before was gone. All the pain and fear and humiliation of the day was gone too. Now she just looked...sad.

"Will you come in with me?" she admitted. "I can't go in there on my own. I know I'll just...I'll go crazy in there if I'm on my own."

It would be cruel to make her go in on her own. But was it really such a good idea for her to go in there? After everything that had happened today, there was no way they could carry on with what was going on between the two of them, was there? And they'd made it pretty clear there was almost no way for the two of them to spend time together alone and keep things purely platonic. They'd tried over and over again, and it had never ended well.

It was late though and Hayley needed her support, so Abs pulled the key out of the ignition and followed Hayley inside.

It was quiet inside, other than the low hum of the refrigerator coming from the kitchen. Gracie's school bag was still on the floor of the hallway by Hayley's shoes, right where she'd left it the last time she'd come home. Hayley spotted it as she was kicking off her trainers, and she froze, staring down at it silently.

"She'll pull through," she said after a few moments, her voice quivering. Maybe if she said it enough times, with

129

enough conviction in her voice, she'd really begin to believe it.

"Why don't I get you a glass of water?" Abs suggested, gently ushering her away from the hallway and into the front room, where she could ease her onto the couch. Hayley sat down, staring across the room at the picture of Gracie from her tenth birthday, with that same distant, hollow expression on her face that Abs had seen before.

"I'll get you that water," Abs said quietly, straightening up to head to the kitchen. Before she could, Hayley's hand shot out, and she grabbed hold of the sleeve of her jacket. Abs was reminded, in a memory that hit her like a sharp blow to the stomach, of the night Hayley had called her to come over after hearing that particularly awful 911 call.

"Don't," she whispered, finally turning her gaze to Abs. She had that same desperate look in her eyes, the same pain and fear as the night Abs had sat beside her and listened to her go over the little girl's 911 call. "Don't go. Just stay here with me, please."

Just like that night, Abs couldn't leave her. The same way she had done before, Abs sat down beside her, and slipped her hand into Hayley's. She didn't know where she stood with Hayley. She had no idea of whether there was going to be anything between them after tonight, but that didn't matter. What mattered was that Hayley needed her.

They sat there in silence for a few moments, before Hayley spoke. Her voice was hoarse and cracked, and it still sounded like it was clogged with tears, but despite that, it still felt good to hear her talk. It made Abs feel a little less alone, like she wasn't just talking into the void.

"Ed…" she began, sniffling. "I don't know how he found out about the accident, but he called me. I guess…maybe the hospital called him?"

"What did he say?" Abs asked, even though she knew from Hayley's reaction back at the hospital that it was likely nothing good.

"He...He just asked what had happened, and when I told him, he said to call him if there were any updates." Hayley shook her head, caught somewhere between disbelief and disgust. "Just that. I asked if he was going to come and see her, and he just...he made up some bullshit excuse about why he couldn't come. Whatever it was, it was a lie, and I know it. He didn't show up to the hospital because it would cut into his drinking time. He's such a selfish piece of shit. His own daughter is in the hospital, and he can't even lift a fucking finger to go see her."

Hayley's shoulder's shook, and she dropped Abs's hand to hide her face as the tears started. She hadn't cried that much since they'd heard the news. She'd just drifted around in that daze which had been so unsettling to look at, but now, away from the hospital, it had all come crashing down on her in one go. The realization of just how awful all this was hit her in one go, and the only thing she could do was sob.

It was a horrible sound. It wasn't the kind of silent crying Abs had seen before, or the light sniffles that followed a stream of tears. Hayley was all but wailing, hunched over with her head towards her knees. Her sobs were broken, a desperate howl of a mother who had no way of helping her only child.

Abs wanted to do something, anything, to take that pain away. She wished she could go back to that morning and grab Gracie by the back of her shirt to stop her from running out. She wished she'd gotten out of bed the night before, before she'd fallen asleep. She wished she could go to the hospital and flip a switch to wake Gracie up, as if nothing had happened.

But she couldn't do any of that. She couldn't *fix* this, no matter how badly she wanted to. She couldn't step back and figure out some logical way out of this, because there was none. There was nothing that either of them could do but sit back and wait to hear from the doctors. So she did the only thing she could do; she wrapped her arms around Hayley's shoulders, and pulled her in close, until the sobbing subsided.

"You know..." she whispered, still wrapped up in Abs's arms. "He was a shitty father to her. He always has been, and even without the alcohol, I think he still would be."

"Who, Ed?"

"Yeah..." Hayley sat up properly, pushing her hair back from her face. She looked at Abs, cocking her head to one side as if she was trying to figure something out. A line appeared between her brows, and then she spoke again. "You know...you're more of a dad to her than what he is."

"I'm more of a *dad*?" Abs echoed.

"You know what I mean. More of a parental figure. You...you care about Gracie. You listen to her, you listen to whatever's bothering her, and you actually try to figure out how to help her. You gave her space to study in your office, you brought her to the gym to try to help her. You...you saw the potential that was there, and you tried your hardest to nurture it. He never did that, not even when she was young."

Abs didn't really know what to say to that. Over the past few months, Hayley had thrown out a lot of mixed signals. First, it was just sex. Sex that wasn't ever supposed to happen but still did, over and over again. Then, she'd felt like things were changing between the two of them, but she just couldn't be sure. By the time she really felt like there might have been something more than sex blossoming between the two of them, Gracie had found them, and it looked like things were over between them.

But she was more of a parental figure to Gracie than her own father? Seriously, what was Abs supposed to say to that? How was that supposed to make her feel?

"Let's get you to bed for a couple hours," she said quietly, standing up. Hayley was so exhausted that she just let Abs scoop her up from the couch, and just silently followed her lead as they went upstairs to the bedroom.

It was strange. They'd been in this position so many times before, but this felt different. They'd fallen into the bedroom, tangled up in each other's arms and just desperate for any kind of contact; they'd walked hand in hand, before passing out in each other's arms; they'd stayed up late into the night, talking about anything and nothing. But not tonight.

Tonight, there was a cold, heavy silence that felt like it was suffocating Abs. She helped Hayley find some pajamas to wear, and tidied up her clothes into the laundry bin, and then once Hayley was under the comforter, she stood there awkwardly. She felt like a stranger in this house, an outlier that didn't belong. It didn't matter how many times she'd come to the house before, or how many hours she'd spent there with Hayley. Tonight, it felt *wrong*.

But as she turned to leave, Hayley reached out for her. "Where are you going?"

After what she'd said earlier, she really wanted Abs to stay?

"I'm...I was *going* to head home," Abs admitted. Hayley's face crumpled though, she looked devastated by the idea of that. "Do you...want me here?"

"I don't want to be alone," she whispered.

Fuck.

Abs was sure she felt a little piece of her heart break with those words. She wanted nothing more than to crawl into bed with Hayley and hold her tightly, whisper to her that everything was going to be okay in the end. But was that what Hayley wanted? Was she really angry with Abs, or did she really want her there? Was she just so fragile that she wanted *anyone*?

Abs sighed, raking a hand through her hair.

"I'll be downstairs," she said finally, taking a small step back from the bed. "I think that's for the best."

"You do?" Hayley whispered.

"Yeah." It was a compromise, the best she could do given the circumstances. It put some distance between them, but she wasn't completely abandoning Hayley. "Get some rest, I'll see you in the morning."

Abs couldn't help but feel a surge of guilt as she left Hayley's bedroom and headed downstairs. She lay on the couch, pulling her jacket over herself like a makeshift blanket. This was for the best, she told herself sternly. Until this was all over, it was best to just be there to support Hayley, but as a friend. After all, it was the fact they had become more than friends that had led to...*to all this.*

Hayley didn't need that. She didn't need the confusion of having to deal with her relationship while she was worrying about Gracie, so for the time being, Abs wasn't going to be— *whatever* she had been over the past few months. She was going to be a friend. That was all.

Abs didn't get much sleep that night. Every time she drifted off, she saw headlights flash in front of her eyes and heard the screech of tires. Someone was screaming around her, and she tasted blood in her mouth. Her seatbelt dug into her chest, making it hard to breathe, and when she looked to her left, Gracie was in the driver's seat. Her head rested on the steering wheel, her eyes were wide and glassy, staring straight at Abs.

And then she'd wake up in a cold sweat, gasping for breath as she clawed at the strap of a seatbelt that wasn't across her chest. It happened over and over again through the night until eventually she woke up and the first weak rays of sunlight filtered into the front room. That was when she gave up trying to sleep, and just lay there in silence.

She couldn't even keep her promise to Hayley that she'd stick around in the morning. She'd promised that she would be there for her when she woke up, but as sunlight streamed through the window, Abs started to feel restless. She couldn't just lay there and wait. The house was too silent, and there was nothing to do. If she stared at the ceiling for too long, the blank canvas would just give way to the mental image of Gracie laying in the hospital bed, with cuts over her face.

Even pacing the living room didn't help. It wasn't enough to stop that restlessness, that sickening anxiety in the pit of her stomach. So instead of waiting for Hayley to wake up, Abs went to the kitchen and wrote a note.

Sorry, I had to nip into work. Call me when you get up and I'll run you to the hospital.

It was a lie. She had the day off, but Hayley probably didn't know that. And besides, she'd probably end up at the gym anyway after a quick shower at home; at least there she could work out and try to take her mind off of everything.

Nineteen

Rather than head home, Abs went straight to the gym. It was just after 5 am. when she unlocked the doors and turned the alarm off. Heading for a bag right in the far corner of the gym, she put her earphones in and started to release the chaos that filled her head. It didn't take long for the rest of the world to dissolve away, melting into the background until the only thing she could see was the bag in front of her.

It had been a long time since she had worked out like this, pushing herself to her very limit. She ignored the burning in her arms that got worse with each punch, ignored how hard her heart was hammering in her chest, ignored how heavy her breathing was. None of that mattered. Not even the familiar ache in her right hand mattered. As long as she stayed there, in front of that bag, punching it over and over again, it was fine. It was—*FUCK*!

Abs misjudged one of her jabs and hit the bag at an odd angle. The fingers of her right hand curled in on themselves sharply, and white hot pain exploded out from her knuckles to her wrist. She cried out in pain, taking a step back from the bag to cradle her hand, as tears sprang to her eyes.

Fuck, fuck, fuck.

Someone was calling her name. She could hear them, distantly, but it was getting a little louder with each passing moment. *Who was that?* God, she couldn't even focus on trying to figure it out. The only thing she could feel was her hand.

"Abs!"

It was Sapphy. It must have been. Fuck, her *hand*.

"Abs, what the hell happened?"

She opened her eyes, looking up at Sapphy's face, and that was when she realized she'd fallen to the floor by the mat. She was curled into a ball, cradling her damaged hand to her chest as if that would possibly help her, and out of the corner of her eye, she saw Logan too.

"What the hell were you thinking?" Sapphy barked. She all but carried Abs out of the main hall and up to her office with Logan getting the door for them.

"Okay..." she said, easing Abs into the sofa against her office wall. "Do you want to tell me what's going on?"

Abs looked up at her old friend and opened her mouth; probably to lie.

"Logan, can you give us a minute?" Sapphy gave a tight smile which Logan returned before leaving them to it.

"I think it's about high time you talked to me. Don't you?"

Abs's instinct was to say that everything was fine, that she had gotten a little too into her workout. She and Sapphy had been friends for far too long though, and she knew there was no way she would buy that. There was no way she could keep this from her for much longer.

Instead of keeping up the lie she and Hayley had sworn themselves to all those months earlier, she told the truth. The problem was, so much had happened in the past few months that she didn't know where to begin.

"Gracie," she said eventually, looking down at her desk. It was easier to do that than to look up at Sapphy's face while she talked. She didn't want to meet her friend's gaze and risk seeing disappointment, or maybe even judgment. "She...she got into an accident. She was hit by a car and ended up in ICU last night."

In her peripheral vision, Abs saw Sapphy drop into the chair across from her. The leather of the seat squeaked under her weight, and she breathed out a heavy sigh. "Jesus Christ...Gracie...Is she okay? Do you know anything?"

"She's not awake right now. There is some swelling on her brain. They expect it to go down, but they aren't sure how long it'll take." Abs swallowed hard and winced as she moved her hand. "She's stable. They just kept saying she is stable, and that's a good thing."

"What happened?"

That was the question she'd been dreading. It was time to come clean about everything. Everything about the relationship she had been hiding from her best friend, everything about the accident. Just…everything.

"Hayley and I…" she began. "We've been seeing each other."

Her palms were sweaty as she spoke. God, how angry was Sapphy going to be that she had lied? How pissed off would Abs be if the tables were turned? Probably very.

But Sapphy didn't look annoyed. She cocked her head to one side, resting her elbow on the armrest of the chair. "For how long?"

"For how long? Is that all you're going to say?"

Sapphy's eyes creased in the corners as she rested her chin against her fist. "How long?"

"A few months. It was…after Gracie's birthday." Abs paused. "Sort of."

"Uh huh…" She nodded.

"I'm sorry I didn't tell you," Abs whispered, wincing as she shifted in her chair and pain shot through her hand. "Hayley—"

"I get it," Sapphy said, cutting across her quickly. "You don't need to explain."

"I don't?"

"I'm not going to lie to you and act like I'm totally cool with you lying to me," Sapphy admitted, leaning back in the chair. "But…I'm assuming you guys had a good reason. And besides, between Gracie ending up in hospital and you fucking your hand up, I think you're dealing with enough right now as it is."

Abs let out a nervous laugh, looking down at her hand. "Yeah, I guess so."

"Don't get me wrong, as soon as that thing heals, we're getting in the ring so I can smack the shit out of you," Sapphy joked. "But that's not what matters right now."

"No, it's not."

"Besides, I'm hardly one to be giving out relationship advice. I'm hardly a role model." Sapphy shrugged and grimaced, causing Abs to let out a pained chuckle. Sapphy's on off relationship with Maura was far from healthy, but as they all knew that was a whole other story. "So what happened with Gracie? How do you and Hayley hooking up get her hit by a car?"

God, Abs felt sick even *thinking* about this again. Picturing the look of shock and horror on Gracie's face as she opened the door on the two of them was just...unbearable.

"She caught us. We both fell asleep, and she walked in. She freaked out and ran out of the house. We started looking for her but...we couldn't...we didn't even know where she'd..."

"Easy," Sapphy said gently, hearing the emotion in Abs's voice. "It's okay."

Abs let out a shaky breath. "When she was running, she got hit by a car. It sent her flying, and she ended up in ICU. She still hasn't woken up."

"Well, shit," Sapphy whispered, shaking her head. "*Shit*."

It wasn't the most eloquent way of summarizing the past couple of days, but it did a good enough job, Abs figured. "Yeah."

"So what now?"

"She's going for another CT scan first thing, and then they'll hope to know more. They suggested Hayley should maybe wait till about lunchtime before going in." Abs sighed, letting all the air in her body flood out.

"Then I think you should take some time off."

Abs looked up sharply at that. "Time off work?"

"Yeah. I mean, you can't train anyone with your hand like that, and besides, this'll give you some time to be with Hayley. Y'know, support her."

"Yeah." Abs didn't want to argue with Sapphy. She didn't want to explain to her that she really just had no idea where she stood with Hayley at the moment, so she figured it was probably just going to be easier to go along with whatever she was suggesting. "Sure."

"You go home." Sapphy stood up. "Take some painkillers, get some rest. I'll sort things out here for you so you don't have to worry about it."

"Are you sure?" Abs asked. "I can just—"

"No," Sapphy said, cutting across her. "Go *home*, Abs. I mean it. You shouldn't be here, not right now."

And that settled it. Once she'd gathered her things and said goodbye to Logan, Abs was headed home. Even though she didn't particularly want to go back to her apartment, she knew there was no arguing with Logan when she was in one of those moods.

Besides, she was probably right anyway.

Abs's apartment was by no means a glamorous one. It was small and kind of shabby compared to what she could afford, but it was in a pretty good neighborhood. The woman across the hall from her sometimes made Baklava, so she had always figured it was a good deal. The other perk that had come with the apartment when she'd moved in was the small balcony overlooking the street.

It wasn't big – there was just enough space for two garden chairs and a little table – but given that Abs had always lived alone, it was more than enough for her. During the summer it gave her a chance to sit outside in the fresh air without having to go to the park, and on mornings when she was up before the sun, she had a place to drink her coffee and watch the sky turn from an inky indigo to a pale, milky blue.

And then, on mornings like this, it gave her somewhere to brood and sulk.

Sapphy had told her to take time off, and while it was probably a good idea that she wasn't going to be training anyone while she was in this state, work would have given her something to take her mind off of everything that had happened over the past couple of days. But sitting here, there was nothing to distract her.

Should I go back to Hayley's apartment? What if she is still sleeping?

When she arrived back home, she stuck the TV on, but even that didn't do much to distract her. It didn't help that her hand was throbbing. She put some ice on it, and while that numbed the pain for a little, it wasn't long before she was looking for something a little stronger. If she could avoid taking painkillers, she would, but this time there would be no choice. They always made her feel tired and at times, a little woozy.

And that was how she found herself lounging on her balcony, with her feet propped up against the railing. With the sun beating down, her eyelids began to grow heavy, and Abs found herself leaning back in her chair lazily. The sound of the street below washed over her as the city began its day, and as she gazed up into the blue sky, a plane passed by.

"Fuck me," she whispered, closing her eyes for a moment. How did things all manage to get twisted up so quickly? How did she go from being wrapped up in Hayley's arms to being dosed up on painkillers with her head being so screwed up?

She already knew the answer to that. The image of Gracie laying in the hospital bed with IV's sticking out of her flashed in Abs's mind's eye. For a few seconds, it was like she was back in that hospital room with her.

Her stomach turned at the thought, and she opened her eyes again with a sigh as her phone started ringing. Hayley's caller ID flashed up on screen, and Abs's stomach twisted again.

God, she wanted to talk to her, but at the same time she didn't. The one thing she knew though was that what Hayley and Gracie needed had to come first just now and everything else could wait. Her feelings, her turmoil, could wait. With a deep breath, she picked up.

"Hey."

"Hi." Hayley's voice was quiet. "How are you doing?"

"Shouldn't I be asking you that question?"

"Probably. I'm okay, given the circumstances. I called this morning. Everything is still the same. They were taking her for her CT scan in an hour."

"Good." Abs sipped her coffee and there was a long pause.

"Why did you leave?" Hayley's voice was hesitant. It was like she wasn't completely sure she wanted to know the answer, but she *needed* to hear it.

"I had to nip into work."

"You said you'd be there when I woke up." Hayley's voice cracked a little.

Fuck. Abs finished her coffee and put it down on the table. Abs knew that she had to tell Hayley the truth.

"Listen…until all this is over, until everything is back to normal, I think…I think we, as in us, should take a step back."

Hayley was quiet for so long that Abs had to check whether she was still on the line. Then she heard a shaky inhale and a sigh.

"A step back?"

"I think it's for the best if I'm just there for you as a friend right now. I think given everything…it's just for the best."

"What if I don't want that?" Hayley asked finally, her voice trembling with emotions. She knew it probably wasn't what Hayley wanted—hell, it wasn't even what *she* wanted, not really. But still, she stuck to it.

"I just think it's for the best."

142

"Okay."

It didn't sound okay. It sounded like Hayley was pissed at her, and Abs couldn't entirely blame her for being angry, but what else was she supposed to do? A day ago she'd said that everything that had happened between the two of them had been nothing but a huge mistake. She'd wanted nothing more to do with Abs, and she'd been adamant about that. But now, had she changed her mind?

"Do you want me to give you a lift to the hospital?" Abs asked as gently as she could.

"No. I'll call an Uber. I'll spend the day with Gracie." The pain in Hayley's voice was evident and Abs wondered if she should insist on taking her, but she thought better of it.

"Okay. Will you let me know how she is doing? Please?"

"Yeah, I'll call you later or maybe tomorrow. I'll see how it goes. Thanks."

There wasn't even a proper goodbye before the call ended.

Twenty

Abs had waited by the phone all day, hoping for Hayley to call with an update, but there was no call. But no matter what was going to happen between them in the long term, the one thing Abs knew was that she wanted to be there as a friend for Hayley.

It was late afternoon when she arrived at the store. Knowing Hayley wouldn't have time to buy groceries, Abs decided to get her some supplies to keep her going. Picking up a mixture of fresh fruit and veg, as well as some quick and easy ready meals, she reckoned she had covered all eventualities. With the bags in the backseat, she made her way up to the hospital.

The same nurse they had spoken to yesterday greeted her as she walked into the ICU unit and as she pushed open the door to Gracie's room, Hayley looked up expectantly as she clutched her daughter's hand.

"Hi, I just wanted to check the two of you were doing okay, or if you needed anything?" Abs asked almost sheepishly.

Hayley smiled at Abs. "I thought you might have been the doctor," she said, giving a small shrug. "We are just waiting to hear what the scans showed. I'm hoping the fact it's been a little while means it is good news."

Abs let the door close behind her.

"You can come in. You can even sit down if you want to." Haley nodded towards the seat next to hers. Abs slipped in next to her, took Hayley's hand, and squeezed it gently.

They sat together quietly for a while, simply watching Gracie. Hayley just seemed glad for the company.

"I was thinking about the stories I used to read to her when she was little. My mom gave her all the Dr Seuss books. *Fox in Socks* was her favorite. It used to make her

144

giggle. Back then, if she was cheeky, you could tickle her into submission. Not like now." Hayley's gaze lay gently on her daughter, watching her chest rise and fall with each breath.

"What was she like when she was small?"

Hayley smiled. "She was a ball of energy, into everything, and she was so happy. All the time. She loved her Nonna. That was my mom. Ed wasn't around much, so Gracie and I would head over to my mom's and spend time there. We moved in with her when Ed and I split up. Gracie loved it. She and my mom used to bake. I'd come back from work and there would always be one treat or another waiting for me. I think I put on a stone in the first few months after we moved in." Hayley laughed, lost in her memory.

Abs was curious about what happened with Hayley's mom, given it was just her and Gracie now, but she felt awkward asking. As if Hayley could sense her question, she carried on.

"We lost my mom a couple of years after that. A massive heart attack. She'd been out with friends when we got the phone call and we rushed up to the hospital, but she was gone by the time we got there."

Hayley's eyes were wet with tears and as Abs squeezed her hand, a tear rolled down her cheek.

"Then it was just me and Gracie against the world. And now—" Hayley shook her head and gazed up at the ceiling as if she was willing, no pleading, for Gracie to be okay.

Before Abs could say anything, the door to the room opened. The doctor dressed in blue scrubs and a white coat walked into the room carrying a large folder. Abs read the name on his badge, Dr. Tim Evans, it declared.

"Ms Campbell, we've had the results back from Gracie's scans and I'm sorry it's taken so long to talk to you, but we had a couple of emergencies earlier today. The swelling on Gracie's brain does seem to be coming down, albeit the improvement is very gradual. While it's potentially good news, we aren't out of the woods yet."

"But its good news. Isn't it?" Hayley was on the very edge of her seat, one hand clutching her daughter, while the other was being held tightly by Abs.

"It is, but we need to keep monitoring the situation. There is still quite a bit of swelling, so I'd say we were cautiously optimistic. It might take more time…"

"How long? Can we expect her to wake up?"

"Ms. Campbell, Gracie—"

"It's Hayley. Just call me Hayley please."

"Hayley, it could be days or even weeks before Gracie wakes. We just need to sit tight and keep monitoring her. I can assure you she is getting the very best of care. We'll run more scans tomorrow, but for now this is the best we can hope for. You need to try to get some rest too, because your daughter is going to need you." His smile was tight, and he gave a quick nod before turning and heading back out of the room.

"It's good news…isn't it?" Hayley's eyes were pleading with Abs for confirmation.

"Yes, the best we could hope for." Abs nodded slowly, hoping it wouldn't take weeks for Gracie to wake up.

* * *

It was late when Abs drove Hayley home. While Hayley showered, Abs unloaded the groceries, cooked a dinner of poached salmon and salad, tidied, tossed clothes in the laundry basket, and gave the place a quick vacuum.

"You didn't have to do all this," Hayley said as she appeared in a robe with her hair wrapped in a fluffy white towel. She looked tired.

146

"It's the least I can do. Now, come and eat."

Hayley played with her food a little, unable to work up much of an appetite due to worrying over Gracie, but she managed to eat a little of the food in front of her. Abs cleared away their plates when they had finished.

"You can call me anytime you want, you know," Abs assured her as she stacked the freshly cleaned dishes in the cupboard. Hayley sat at the kitchen island, nursing a cup of coffee. The towel that she'd wrapped around her dark hair was starting to slip off, but she didn't seem to care much. She was just staring into space, her eyes unfocused.

"Yeah."

Her voice didn't even sound like her own. It was distant, cold, like she was speaking to a stranger, and it hurt to hear. But Abs knew she didn't have any right to demand anything else from Hayley, not after everything that had happened.

"I actually took some time off work," Abs explained gently. "So I'm yours whenever you need me. If you need me to give you a ride to the hospital, or get you more groceries…anything, just ask."

"Thank you."

Hayley didn't want to talk, and Abs could see that. She offered to freshen up her coffee, or make them lunch, but Hayley told her she was fine in that same hollow, lifeless voice. Eventually, Abs just gave up and said goodbye, taking the spare set of keys that Hayley had given her when she left.

That was how the rest of the week went. Abs would run Hayley to and from the hospital, and help out with anything that needed doing at the house. She would clean up anything that was lying around, do the dishes, wash and fold the laundry. She would make sure the fridge was fully stocked, or order them some dinner, and she would try to make small talk with Hayley to take her mind off of everything.

And Hayley would respond in that same quiet, monotone voice. Sometimes she would talk about Gracie, or maybe comment on the show they were watching, but that was it.

147

She never talked about *them,* and neither did Abs. Neither of them really wanted to bring it up, because they were worried that they might not like where the conversation would lead.

Abs didn't want to lose her. She was so scared that one day Hayley would just turn around and tell her to leave, and the thought of that happening was almost too much to bear. However, the bigger thought that was even harder to bear was the fact that Hayley still hadn't regained consciousness.

* * *

A week after the accident, Abs woke to her phone ringing on the beside table. She pushed her hand out from where it was buried under the comforter and blindly scrabbled for it before bringing it to her ear.

"Yeah?" she grunted, her voice gravelly from sleep.

Normally her phone was on silent, but since Gracie had been taken to the hospital, she'd started putting it on the loudest possible setting, just in case there was an emergency in the middle of the night. So far that week, she'd been woken up by two cold callers and a text from her mom about a skateboarding dog.

"Abs?"

She shot up in bed at the sound of Hayley's voice, and the fog of sleep that clouded her head dissipated. Her room was still dark, which meant it must have been early, and she knew Hayley wouldn't call at that hour unless it was something important.

"Hayley? What's wrong? Are you okay?"

"The hospital called." Her voice was faint, like something was covering her mouth. "Gracie…"

Abs felt sick. There were any number of things that could have happened to her in that hospital bed, and most of them weren't exactly things she wanted to think about. She squeezed her eyes shut, trying to calm her breathing, but it didn't work.

"Yeah?"

"She woke up. They called, and she's...she's awake. She's okay."

Perhaps it was the fact that she was still half asleep, or maybe it was just the shock of the news, but it took Abs a few seconds to process that information. Gracie had woken up. She was going to be okay.

It was okay.

"I'm getting dressed." She threw the comforter off and practically fell out of bed, before stumbling over to the dresser against the far wall of her room. "I'll be there soon, and then I'll drive you over to the hospital, okay?"

"Okay." Hayley's voice trembled on the other end of the line, and Abs realized that she must have been crying. "Please hurry."

"Of course. I'll be there as soon as I can." Abs hung up the phone without a proper goodbye and started scrabbling around in her drawers for clean clothes to wear.

Gracie was okay.

Gracie was okay.

Gracie was okay.

That was the only thought going through her mind, like an echoing chorus over and over again. She wasn't even paying attention to where she was going, not really. Instead, she was moving on autopilot, grabbing her keys and her jacket, then ran to the underground parking lot of her building. It didn't matter that she probably woke her neighbor when she slammed her front door. It didn't matter that she drove straight through a stop sign without even slowing down. It didn't even matter that she probably broke every speed limit on her way to Hayley's place.

The only thing that mattered was that Gracie was okay.

Twenty-One

By the time they arrived at the hospital, Gracie had already been moved out of ICU and into a ward room on the floor above. The two of them rushed through the halls together, desperately searching for her room, but when they found it they both stopped dead in their tracks for a moment. As they hovered by the door, Abs couldn't help the same nerves that she'd felt the first time they'd come to the hospital together. No matter how hard she tried, she just couldn't shake that mental image of Gracie laying in the hospital bed, surrounded by machines that were keeping her alive.

When they opened the door, Gracie was sitting upright in bed, propped up by some pillows. There was an empty lunch tray beside her, so clearly she wasn't doing too badly. When she saw them walk in, she looked over with a grin, and waved with her good arm.

"Mom!"

A surge of relief flooded through Abs at the sight of Gracie awake, and as they reached the bed, her knees went weak. She held onto the railing at the foot of the bed for support, and for a moment, she thought she'd actually blacked out. Her vision went a little spotty, but then Hayley's choked sob of relief brought her back.

"Oh Gracie…" she whispered tearfully, rushing to her daughter's bedside. "Look at you…oh baby…"

"You two look like shit," she croaked, managing a weak grin which Abs returned.

"Hey, we didn't need to come all the way over here," Abs joked, nudging Hayley gently. "She's fine. Look at her."

"God, I'm never letting you out of my sight. Never, ever again, you hear me?" Hayley said, brushing hair back from Gracie's face to look at her properly.

She was looking a lot better than what she had been when they'd first gone to see her up in ICU. The scrape on her forehead still stood out, a stark contrast against her skin, but thankfully most of the other scrapes were beginning to fade. Her arm was still in the cast and held up with a bandage. No doubt she'd be in a lot of pain once the morphine drip wore off, but despite that, she seemed to have walked off relatively unscathed.

It could be worse, Abs reminded herself, with a wry smile.

"How's the arm?" she asked, motioning to Gracie's cast.

"I asked the nurse, but they won't put a metal pin in." Gracie sighed, looking down at it. "It's only fractured in one place."

"Only?" Hayley winced. "Abby—"

"I wanted a cool scar!" she protested, pointing at Abs. "Like hers! I got hit by a car and I don't even have the scars to show it!"

"We drove here." Abs perched on the edge of the bed, down by Gracie's feet. "If you want, we can wheel you out into the parking lot and go for round two."

"Stop it!" Hayley whined, gathering Gracie into her arms and cradling her to her chest. "Both of you, that's enough. God, I feel like I'm about to have a heart attack. Do you know how badly you scared me?"

"I know, Mom," Gracie said quietly. "I'm sorry, I really am. I didn't mean to—"

"To what? Get hit by a car?" Hayley fussed, touching her index finger to the side of Gracie's head lightly, right where there was a scratch. "Look at your face…"

"Mom, I'm really fine!" Gracie giggled, trying to wriggle out of her arms. "Stop!"

The two of them started laughing as Hayley eased herself onto the bed, cuddling Gracie tightly and promising her that she was never going to let her go. Abs sat there for a few moments at the edge of the bed, before standing up and slipping out of the door to give them some privacy. Neither of them seemed to notice her leave.

She was glad Gracie was okay, glad that her injuries were pretty much just superficial, but as the door closed behind her, she couldn't help but feel just a little twinge of sadness too.

Hayley had needed her after the crash, and she knew that. She'd needed a ride to the hospital. She'd needed a hand to hold when she'd walked to ICU, and she'd needed someone with her when she was in the blind panic after they'd left. And Abs had been more than happy to provide all of that for her, but that reunion back there had been a *family* reunion, between a mother and a daughter. She couldn't help but feel as though she'd been intruding on them just by being there.

As much as she'd tried to insert herself into things over the past few months, she wasn't a part of their family. Of course, she'd known that all along, but as things between her and Hayley had gotten more serious, there had been just a little part of her that had hoped *maybe, just maybe*, she had a little place by their sides. Even with everything that had happened, she still felt like an interloper on the sidelines.

Maybe she could get a coffee while she waited for them. She could certainly do with a pick-me-up. She'd barely started walking towards the cafeteria though, when she heard the door open, and as she turned back to look at it, she saw Hayley slip out into the hall.

"Gracie wants to talk to you," she said quietly. Her voice was still a little stuffy from tears, and her eyes were puffy and red rimmed, but when she met Abs's gaze, she smiled. It was a weak, exhausted smile, but it was good enough for her.

"She wants to talk to me?"

"Yeah."

Abs looked back at the door, before glancing at Hayley again, just to make sure.

"Why?"

152

"Go in and talk to her. I'm going to get some water from the vending machine."

Abs expected her to just walk off, but Hayley did something that took her by surprise. She reached down, slipped her hand into Abs's, and squeezed her fingers gently, before kissing her cheek.

"Go in," she said gently, smiling. "It's okay."

What was that? Was that gratitude? Was that a 'thanks for getting me here' kiss? A 'thank you for being here' kiss? Something more? Something less? Now wasn't the time to worry about that. Abs looked at the door to Gracie's room. This *was what was important*. Gracie was okay, she was alive and (mostly) unhurt. And more than that, she wanted to see her.

Of course, there was always the chance that she wanted to scream at Abs again. Her stomach tightened into knots at the very thought of that, and although she was nervous about talking to Gracie alone for the first time since the fight, Abs forced herself to open the door.

Gracie was still sitting up in bed when she walked in, closing the door behind her. Abs approached her slowly, almost like she was worried that a sudden movement would set the girl off again.

"Hey there, kiddo."

Abs's could hear her own voice sounding tight, strained, and clogged up with tears. When she swallowed, her throat felt like there was something pressing down on it.

In all the time she and Hayley had been seeing each other, she had imagined telling Gracie about them so many times. But never, not in a single one of those scenarios, had she imagined it would go like this. She figured maybe they would sit Gracie down after dinner and explain quietly and gently that over the past few months they had developed feelings for each other. In an ideal world, there would have been less yelling, fewer surprises, and no one would have ended up in hospital.

153

Admittedly, Gracie didn't *look* pissed, which was good, but it didn't really help Abs feel any less on edge. There was no way to hide or lie about all this now, since Gracie had caught them in such a compromising position. It was all out there in front of them now. The only thing left to do was to *talk* about it.

"Hey." Gracie propped herself up on her pillows a bit more, smiling.

"Your mom said you wanted to talk to me?" Abs hovered by the foot of the hospital bed, uncertain about getting any closer to her.

"Yeah." Gracie tugged on the bedsheets around her, suddenly looking a little uncomfortable.

This was it. There was no turning back now; they had to talk about what had happened before. Abs felt her stomach twist into knots as she waited for Gracie to speak again. Was she going to get angry again? Scream? Tell her to stay away?

"I'm sorry for freaking out like that back at home," she said finally, sighing. "Yelling at you guys and running out like that. Mom said that I really scared you guys."

"You did," Abs admitted, rubbing the back of her neck. "But…to be honest, I can't really blame you for reacting the way you did. I don't know how well I would have handled it if I had been in your place."

"I'm not mad that you and my mom are like…a thing," she said quickly. "I actually think it's kind of cool, really."

Abs let out the breath she hadn't even realized she'd been holding in. It came out as a strained, nervous chuckle; a sound of weak relief. "Really?"

"Yeah." The corner of Gracie's mouth twitched, but before it could become a proper smile, it was gone. "I *am* kind of mad you guys didn't tell me about all this though."

Abs winced at that. It was fair, she had every right to be pissed about being kept out of the loop, and as much as Abs had tried to justify their secrecy, deep down she knew it. She felt the same surge of guilt come over her that she'd felt after

154

telling Sapphy about everything. There was that look of disappointment in her eyes that was so much worse than anger or frustration. In fact, Abs kind of wished she was yelling again. "Yeah. I...I kind of figured you would be. And I'm sorry, Gracie. I really am."

"Why didn't you tell me? Did you guys think you couldn't trust me?" Gracie frowned. "If you guys had wanted me to keep it a secret, I wouldn't have told anyone, I swear."

It was difficult to explain all this to Gracie without turning around and blaming all the secrecy and sneaking around on Hayley. After all, she was the one who had asked for them to stay low key the entire time. But despite that, Abs knew it wasn't fair to push all of this on her. After all, she'd had her reasons for handing things the way she had done.

"Dating when you're a parent...it's hard," Abs said eventually, finally easing herself down to perch on the edge of the bed. Gracie didn't seem like she was going to lash out and toss her out of the room any time soon, so she felt comfortable enough to sit down while they talked. "And I think...I think your mom was worried. She didn't want you to get hurt."

"Worried?" Gracie echoed. "About me?"

"This relationship between your mom and me, it was a lot more complicated than most relationships. Your mom had a lot to figure out, especially right at the start. It was hard for her."

"Yeah, she told me that. She said she's always kind of known she was...y'know."

"Gay," Abs interjected, with a smile. It had been a long time since she'd spent time with someone who had that immature, adolescent fear of the word, as if it was some kind of curse word. "You can say it. It's fine."

Gracie shot her a sheepish smile before carrying on. "She says she has always kind of known that she was a lesbian, but she sort of—pushed it down for a really long time."

"She was worried about a lot of things, but coming out was one of the big ones, yeah. And I think she wanted to try to figure out our relationship before telling you about it. She didn't want to make a big deal out of this relationship only to have it fall apart after a few months. That wouldn't have been fair for you."

Gracie nodded slowly, looking down at the bedsheets. It was a lot to take in, so Abs wasn't surprised she needed a couple minutes of silence. Eventually, she looked up and met Abs's gaze again.

"Do you think it's going to fall apart?" she asked.

After everything that had happened to them, Abs honestly wasn't sure of how to answer that question. A week ago she would have said 'no' without even having to think about it. But today, she just didn't know. She knew what she *wanted*, but she just wasn't sure of what Hayley wanted.

"I hope not."

It was the most honest answer she could come up with, the most diplomatic one too, given how uncertain everything was.

"My mom said the same thing," Gracie admitted.

"She did?" Abs tried to keep the excitement, the desperation, out of her voice, but it was hard. She knew that she probably ended up sounding like a middle schooler who'd been told her crush liked her back. "What did she say? Like *exactly*?"

"She said things between the two of you had been going super well, and that she was really happy with you until..." Gracie trailed off and smiled sheepishly. "Well, like...you know."

"And now?"

"And now...she said things have been kind of weird between the two of you, which she doesn't like. She said you fought, and she said some things she didn't mean..."

Another surge of guilt came over Abs. She'd figured that she had been doing Hayley a favor by keeping her distance over the past week, but in reality she'd probably only made things worse. It had just given her another thing to worry about.

Abs knew that she should apologize, and she *wanted* to apologize to her, but when Hayley poked her head back inside the door a few moments later, she knew it wasn't the right time or place. Instead, she just smiled over at her, and beckoned her inside. They sat there together, side by side on the edge of Gracie's bed until the nurses finally kicked them out a few hours later.

Twenty-Two

Abs kept re-running the afternoon's conversations through her head. As they sat in the car together on their drive home, she opened her mouth once or twice to apologize, but her palms would grow sweaty against the wheel and she'd chicken out. Eventually, she just put the radio on to fill the silence. It wasn't until she'd parked in her usual space outside Hayley's house and walked her all the way up to her door that she gathered up the courage to do it.

Hayley opened the front door and flicked on the hall light. She turned to Abs with a small, almost shy smile – the kind Abs hadn't seen since they'd first started seeing each other – clutching the strap of her purse with both hands. "Do you…do you want to come in for a bit?"

"Yes," Abs said, far too quickly for her to even try to be cool about it. There was no point in lying about it anymore. The only thing she wanted to do was follow Hayley inside and wrap her arms around her. It was the only thing she'd wanted to do all week.

"Come on," Hayley said, beckoning her closer. "Come on in."

Abs didn't need convincing. She followed Hayley inside and let the door swing shut behind her.

"You want something to drink?" Hayley was already heading towards the kitchen. She didn't bother turning on the overhead lights as she walked in. Instead, she just used the dim glow of the hall light to guide her.

"After the week we've had? I think we've earned it." Abs shot her a wry smile, instantly feeling guilty. She knew that the week hadn't just been shitty because of what had happened to Gracie. During all of it, she hadn't exactly been of much comfort to Hayley.

"I was thinking the same thing." Hayley grabbed two glasses from the cupboard and poured them each a generous serving of wine.

"Thanks." Abs took her glass, staring down into it for a few moments. It was easier to focus on the rippling of the drink inside – such a dark shade of red that was almost black – rather than look up.

She had to apologize. There was no use putting it off any longer, and Abs knew it.

"I've been an asshole the last week or so," she said quietly, looking up slowly. Hayley was in the far corner of the kitchen, still leaning against the counter. The hallway light didn't really stretch that far into the kitchen, so as she stood there, she was cast mostly in shadow. Abs couldn't even make out her facial expression, she couldn't tell whether she was angry.

"What makes you say that?" Hayley asked. Her voice was even and completely calm. There wasn't a hint of emotion there that could give away how she was really feeling.

"You needed me this week." Abs sighed and put her wine down on the countertop. "You needed me to be there for you, and I wasn't."

"You took me to the hospital. You cooked, cleaned. You were there," Hayley reminded her.

"That's not what I mean."

"No. I know it's not." She paused, and in the darkness, Abs made out her silhouette as she took a drink.

"I thought I was doing you a favor," Abs admitted. "After what you said when Gracie ran off, I thought you…needed a friend. You didn't need whatever it was that I was to you. I tried to just keep things platonic, because I was worried that if things went any further, you'd end up regretting it after everything settled down."

"I didn't mean what I said, you know," Hayley told her gently. "I was angry and scared. I was scared I was going to

159

lose Gracie, and I took it out on you, but I never meant any of it."

"I know." It sounded kind of stupid to Abs now. Of course, Hayley had just been angry; she'd been out of her mind with worry, and she blamed Abs for it because she was the closest person to her at that moment. "But I felt like if I let things go any further while you were so worried about Gracie...I was worried I'd just be taking advantage of you, with the way you were."

Abs wouldn't have blamed Hayley if she didn't understand; it wasn't like she was explaining herself very clearly. But she had really felt like she was doing the right thing at the time.

"I'm sorry," Abs whispered.

Hayley was silent for a moment, and then Abs heard the clink of her glass rest on the countertop. Hayley slowly made her way over, crossing the kitchen to come face to face with Abs.

The light from the hallway was much stronger here, and as Hayley got close, Abs realized that there were tears in her eyes. Her hands itched to reach out and pull her into a hug, but she stopped herself. Before she did anything like that, she wanted to hear what Hayley had to say.

"I'm sorry too," she whispered. Her voice shook a little, and she sniffled before continuing. "I never meant what I said when Gracie ran off, and when we came back from the hospital, I guess I thought that I was making it clear that I didn't mean it. When you started pulling away from me, I thought I'd hurt you. I thought you wanted to end things, and I just...I didn't know what to do. I couldn't deal with everything all at once."

Abs let out the breath she hadn't realized she was holding in, then shook her head.

"God...we're ridiculous."

Hayley laughed tearfully, sniffling again. She blinked, and the tears that had been welling in her eyes finally spilled over. They caught in her lashes and splashed down her cheeks, leaving wet tracks against her skin. Finally, Abs reached over and smeared them away with her thumb, before leaning in closer and kissing her.

"I missed you," Abs whispered, burying her face into the crook of Hayley's neck. "I know I've been around, I know we've seen each other, but I've *missed* you."

"I know," Hayley whispered. She wrapped her arms around Abs tightly, pulling her in as close as humanly possible. After the week the two of them had gone through, she never wanted to have to let go again. "We're both kind of stupid, huh?"

"We're both *very* stupid," Abs agreed, laughing. "Let's not do this again. Ever."

"Agreed." Hayley pulled back so she could look Abs in the eye. "From now on, let's just be honest. No more hiding anything."

Hiding.

Hiding.

Abs's heart sank when she realized the one other thing she hadn't yet told Hayley. "Sapphy knows, and probably Logan too. Sorry."

"She does? They do?"

"I...the day after we saw Gracie in ICU, I went to the gym..." Abs paused, sighing. "I wasn't in a good place, and she could tell. I ended up telling her about us."

To her surprise, Hayley didn't look upset with her. Instead, she smiled. "Well, I suppose that's a good start. Gracie knows...Sapphy knows...maybe Logan. Who else should we tell?"

"Are you...you mean that?" Abs's smile was so wide that her jaw was probably going to hurt in the morning, but she didn't care. "You want to—"

"I want people to know about us." Hayley nodded, reaching up to fiddle with Abs blonde quiff. "I want to walk down the street holding your hand. I want to go on dates with

161

you. I want to tell everyone I've found someone I'm happy with, someone I want to spend my life with. If this has taught me anything, it's that we never should have kept this a secret."

"Yeah, I think we both screwed up a little with that," Abs admitted, with a small smile. "But—if you're really okay with telling people…I'd like that. I'd really, really like that."

"So starting tomorrow, no more secrets, no more sneaking around." Hayley grinned. She looked excited, but equally a little nervous too.

They grabbed the wine and headed to the front room to celebrate this new milestone. Abs leaned back on the sofa and raised her arm, allowing Hayley to snuggle up against her.

"Can I kiss you?" Hayley's voice was almost a whisper.

"Of course you can kiss me. You don't have to ask."

Hayley brushed her lips, then looked up into Abs's eyes as she did. Small, delicate, tentative kisses grazed against Abs's mouth and a feeling of warmth lit up in her chest. It wasn't the thrust of lust cascading through her body, it was something much rounder, fuller; something that seemed to fill her completely. The kiss deepened but slowly, without the necessity to rush. These weren't stolen moments which could be snatched away from them. The time was now theirs, and they had all the time in the world.

"Do you want the rest of that wine?" Abs eyes held a mischievous glint. "Or can I take you to bed just now? I mean, it's been a long week and well, you look a little tired."

"Really? Does that normally work for you? Telling a woman she looks a bit rough?" Hayley grabbed a cushion and swung it at Abs.

"Whoa!" Abs chuckled. "You can't blame me for trying."

"If you want to take me to bed…just ask. It's that easy."

"Hayley, you have never been easy, but you've always been worth it." Abs squeezed Hayley's hand. "Now do you want to race each other to the bedroom or can I just grab you and throw you over my shoulder, cave woman style?"

"Why don't I take you?" Hayley stood, pulling Abs up with her. Without another word, she led Abs through to the bedroom.

There was no rush to strip, instead they took their time to undress each other. Kisses and tender touches punctuated the discarding of each piece of clothing. Fingertips explored exposed skin, brushing, gliding, provoking until need consumed their every fiber.

Hayley threw back the comforter, drawing Abs down onto the bed with her.

"I want you to sit on my face." Hayley smiled coyly. "I want to taste you."

"Okay." Abs watched as Hayley lay down. "But how about this—" Instead of straddling Hayley's body and facing her, Abs kneeled on either side of her body, facing away. "Because then I can—" Leaning forward, Abs lowered her face to Hayley's center, inhaling her scent, before sliding her tongue between lips to reach her engorged clit.

A gasp, followed by a low moan, filled the room as Hayley signaled her approval. Abs smiled, suddenly aware of warm hands on her hips, which seemed intent on drawing her own center towards the warm breath beneath.

"Hmm—oh—I like that," Abs murmured. Allowing herself to drop back further, she felt Hayley's tongue tease its way over her center. An involuntary rocking of her hips allowed for deeper pleasure and a wave of warm excitement washed over her body.

Resting a forearm on either side of Hayley, Abs placed her lips around Hayley's clit, sucking her in. A swirl of her tongue, glancing over the hard nub, caused Hayley's hips to buck. The air filled with low groans, moans and whimpers of delight as they took their time in pleasuring each other; getting lost in waves of intoxicating sensation.

163

Each flick, swirl and delve of tongue and lips brought them closer and closer to the pique of arousal: A slow, momentous crescendo of unbridled passion was about to be unleashed. The exquisite struggle between the desire to never leave the moment and the hunger for release had to reach its inevitable conclusion and with strangled screams and guttural anguish orgasms took hold. First Hayley, then Abs, surrendered themselves to the carnal crash of sensations that overtook their bodies.

Panting and covered in sweat, Abs recovered her limp body to lie next to Hayley, bringing her face so close, their noses touched.

"You taste incredible," Hayley murmured

"So do—" Abs words were lost to the kiss which Hayley placed on her lips. There was depth and a sincerity to the embrace which left Abs speechless when Hayley finally pulled back.

"You are incredible, Abby. *You* make *me* feel—" Hayley's smile was so wide it literally covered the width of her face. "incredible. Gracie is going to be okay and I've…got *you*." Hayley let out a long, satisfied sigh. "I want to tell everyone."

Abs laughed, returning the smile in equal measure but with one correction that just had to be made.

"But less of the Abby, ok?"

"I'll call you whatever you ask if you keep me feeling this good." Hayley laughed snuggling her face into Abs's neck.

With arms wrapped around each other they fell into a contented sleep. It was going to be okay. Better than okay.

Epilogue

Considering the fact that she had been hit by a car, Gracie got off lightly. After a few more days in hospital she was allowed to come home, where she was welcomed back by Abs, Hayley, and a few of her friends. There was some physiotherapy in the months that followed the crash, but it was nothing that she couldn't handle, and she was back to spending most afternoons at the gym before the end of the year. Sapphy and Logan, as well as Abs, looked out for her and she became almost a permanent fixture. Sapphy even gave her a job helping out during the holidays.

But only a few months later everyone was back at the hospital, but this time it wasn't Gracie that was being treated, but Abs. It turned out there was an infection in one of the pins. That had been the reason why she'd been struggling with pain for so long. She probably would have gone on ignoring it until it was too late to fix it, but Hayley, Gracie, and Sapphy put up a united front and all but forced her to go and see a doctor. After another operation to fix the hand, she was sent home with some fresh pins, and a set of strict instructions about not straining herself.

Perhaps it was that doctor's note which pushed Hayley to make the suggestion she made. Perhaps it was just a convenient excuse, but when she drove Abs back from the hospital after her operation, she casually brought up the idea of Abs moving in.

"Like…permanently?" Abs asked, cocking an eyebrow.

"I know it's quite quick," Hayley admitted. "But think about it. You spent more time at our place than you do at your own. Half of your stuff is here anyway, and I know that Gracie would love to have you there, plus you'd be closer to work and—"

She stopped talking as she caught sight of Abs grinning in the passenger seat.

"What are you smiling about?"

"Did you plan out a speech or something?"

"No! I just thought that it was…I mean, especially with your hand."

Abs smiled at her as Hayley's cheeks turned pink. "I think we should do it."

"You do?" She seemed surprised.

"Yeah. You made a good argument. What can I say?"

Hayley chuckled, turning her attention back to the road. "Well, I *am* the smartest woman of the house."

"Gracie takes a close second, don't worry." Abs paused. "Do you think she'll like the idea of me moving in?"

The corner of Hayley's mouth twitched into a smile, and she glanced at Abs out of the corner of her eye. "Something tells me she'll be fine with it."

"Something?" Abs echoed. "What's that supposed to mean?"

"I might have brought the idea up to her." Hayley shrugged. "She *might* have been over the moon about the whole thing. So y'know, it's probably a good thing that you're on board with the whole idea."

Abs grinned, leaning back in her seat as she looked over at Hayley. She'd changed so much since they'd first met. Sure, she was still stressed from her job, overworked and underpaid, but she seemed happier now. When she came home after a long shift at work, her eyes lit up at the sight of Abs and Gracie watching a film together, and she'd run to join them. She laughed more often, made more jokes, and even some of her friends had noticed the change in her. Abs wondered if *she* had changed at all over the past few months. She'd have to ask Sapphy and Logan.

"You know something?"

"What?" Hayley glanced over at her and caught sight of the grin on her lips.

"I can't *believe* you slapped me the second time we met."

Thank You

Thank you for reading Inside fighter, I hope you enjoyed the book and if you did, I'd love it if you could leave a review.

If you would like to contact Ruby about this or any of her other books, she can be contacted at RubyScott.author@gmail.com

Alternatively you can sign up for her newsletter;

https://mailchi.mp/578501699a88/welcome-to-rubys

About the Author

Ruby Scott was always an avid reader of#lesfic and lesbian romance and one day she got up had an extra cup of coffee and thought "I'm going to have a shot at writing a story." Her books, she jokes, are always a result of an extra cup of coffee. Born to a British parents, Ruby has lived in many places and loves travelling when it's possible. She never goes anywhere without her Laptop and her best pal, Baxter.

www.rubyscott.com

Also by Ruby Scott

Printed in Great Britain
by Amazon

61684999R00102